WHISPERS

At first there seemed nothing to mar Persis' happiness. The man whom she had wed with such joyful eagerness more than fulfilled her dreams. Anything she wanted he granted—clothes, jewelry, cars, and above all those things, the essential gift of his captivating charm and intense passion.

How could she ever have loved another? How could anyone fail to fall under his spell?

Why then did his own mother shrink from his touch? Why did the local villagers avoid him? Why did his own servants look at him with barely masked fear?

And again and again Persis remembered the whispers she once had laughed at: *"He is a devil, and his family is accursed . . ."*

The Curse of Carranca

Elsie Lee

A DELL BOOK

Published by
DELL PUBLISHING CO., INC.
1 Dag Hammarskjold Plaza
New York, New York 10017
Reprinted by arrangement with the author.
Dell ® TM 681510, Dell Publishing Co., Inc.
Printed in the United States of America
First Dell printing—June 1973

chapter 1

Some girls join the Peace Corps, or the Young Republicans; I knew one who took a Berlitz course in Russian when she was jilted. I like to be different. I went to Portugal.

Strictly speaking, I was never left at the altar. It was worse than that. It turned out I'd never been engaged and had been wearing the Greenwich Village zircon on the wrong finger for months. As Artie retorted when Laura called him a ratfink at Trentini's, "Come off it, all I said was, it matched her eyes. Did I tell her where to wear it?"

"If you were anything *but* a ratfink," Laura stated, "you would have *told* her, instead of smugly drifting along, letting everyone think you were going to marry Persis—and I only hope Poochy's a better cook than Persis, or you'll have the worst of the deal all the way round."

Poochy then slapped Laura, leading immediately to a joyous free-for-all, in which Rab hung a mouse on Artie, who caromed into Ann, knocking her new bridgework to the floor, where Tom stepped on it disastrously, while socking Poochy's roommate's boy friend . . . and so on and so forth. It was a most satisfactory donnybrook; everybody, even complete strangers, got into the act. The floor was swimming in beer from overturned mugs, and Patrolman Keoghan slid onto his overweight fanny in the very act of collaring Artie . . . but the high point of the fracas was a scalp lock torn by Laura from Poochy's pony tail, proving beyond a shadow of a doubt what presumably only her hairdresser had known for sure.

Six telephone calls next morning gave me all the happy details. "If only you'd been there, it was an absolute wowser!" Laura mourned. "Where were you anyway, Persis? We waited and waited."

"I went to the Hunter College subscription series, it was Segovia," I said, shakily, closing my memory to mousy Miss Adelman sitting ecstatically in Artie's usual seat beside me. "I didn't get home until nearly one."

"Oh, it was over by then," she said, regretfully. "We were at the police station, so you missed everything. What a shame!"

"Yes, wasn't it?" I gulped and used the secretarial excuse. "Have to go—the boss just buzzed. . . ."

But by the time Marco Trentini called, I was totally unnerved. "Please, I'm so sorry, Marco," I pleaded. "I never dreamed they'd start fighting on my account . . . so unnecessary, I knew all about the marriage. . . ."

Which was a damn lie. I hadn't known a thing, nor even suspected, until I got back a day early from a holiday week at home, and came face to face with Artie and Poochy at a Village street fair. To do him justice, he changed color but owned up at once. "Persis, didn't expect you back until tomorrow—what luck to run into you—wanted you to be first to know Poochy and I are married! I knew you were out of town . . . couldn't tell you beforehand, we just up and decided to Do It," he said, a bit too heartily. "We stuck a note in your box to call soon as you got back."

It was true I'd found a note. I'd called and got no answer. Poochy's eyes were watchful, waiting to see how I'd react, her hand sliding proprietarily through Artie's elbow—and *she'd* got a proper diamond with a substantial gold band beneath. I pulled myself together, blinking with exaggerated double-take. "Darlings, how *wonderful*—if jet-propelled!" I said, merrily, patting Artie's arm and depositing a kiss on Poochy's cheek. "The best of luck! As soon as the smoke clears, come for dinner?"

His face cleared with relief. "Great! Hey, who you with? By yourself? Come along with us!"

"Thanks, no—I'm looking for Ann and Tom. They'll be hanging over one of the jewelry booths. I don't want to stay late, anyway—had to wait an *hour* for a third section of the Boston shuttle," I said, dramatically, "because I missed the four o'clock. I'm for home and bed, as soon as I've glanced about. Have fun, and keep in touch."

"Will do," Artie assured me, dropping Poochy's arm and heading to the ring-toss for a caged parrakeet. "Hey, baby, you still want one of these things? Here goes!" While he was paying for the rings, taking a dashing stance and tossing for the center spindle, Poochy looked at me. "I'm—sorry, Persis," she said, odiously sad and wide-eyed.

"For what, darling?" I inquired, amazed. "When love surfs in, why yell for a lifeguard? I only wish I'd known you wanted a parrakeet—you could have had the one he won for me last year. I had to give it away because of my cat. Dear boy," I murmured, affectionately, "how he does love rings! Oh, look," excitedly, "I believe he's got it! Take a blue one, Poochy, they're the most intelligent. Probably even you can teach it to talk when you have time. Well, so long."

Her eyes narrowed sharply, half furious, half bewildered. "You act like you don't give a damn. Okay, but we aren't going to be palsy-walsy. Don't bother to ask us for dinner, we'll have a previous engagement."

"That makes two of us," I said, sweetly, "and just to ease your conscience—if any—I really don't give a damn. He's much more your speed than mine." I turned and blindly lost myself in the crowd moving sluggishly along Fourth Street, twisting and sliding around the groups clustered at display booths, walking in the street when necessary, until finally I was home.

Scant comfort to remember Poochy's incredulity, the tinge of disappointment when I hadn't given her any opening for bitchery. I was equally incredulous, sliding the zircon from my finger and hurling it violently into a corner of the room, before bursting into tears. Between Wassermann tests, getting a license and a three-day waiting period, you can't get married on the spur of the moment in New York these days. I knew it. They'd had to plan ahead. Why hadn't he said so?

All these past weeks, he'd been dropping into Trentini's, Quags, our usual haunts, being part of the gang, going to the concerts with me (I'd paid for the subscription, he took me to dinner first), letting everyone accept us as an engaged couple, automatically invited together. Not a sight, sound or smell of Poochy—who wasn't part of the inner circle anyway, because she lived up-

town to be nearer modeling jobs. And all the time . . .
all the time . . .

I dried my eyes, drearily blew my nose and sat up,
aware of a peculiar metallic rattle. "Shadrach?"

"Mrraur?" he said—which apparently means yes in
cat-language. He came trotting out of the corner with
the zircon in his mouth, to drop it at my feet. We both
looked at it for a silent moment. Then Shadrach extended a deft black paw and batted it gently. In the
lamplight, it glimmered faintly; Shadrach crouched
contemplatively. After a second, he sat up and batted the zircon toward the lamp in a small shower of
blue glitter. Then he sprang after it and killed it to the
entire satisfaction of both of us. Finally he neatly
fielded it back to my toes with one swipe, and inquired, "Hrrroooo?"

I looked at the zircon. If Artie'd paid more than
fifty bucks, he'd been stung—but he hadn't. I suddenly
remembered it'd come from Ann and Tom's shop. I'd
bet they let him have it at cost, or about twenty dollars.
I thought vaguely of two home-cooked dinners a week
for nearly a year . . . and Poochy's diamond that had
cost at least a thousand.

Shadrach stalked forward and eyed me commandingly. "Wauuurrrr?"

"All right," I said, "you may have it to play with."
It seemed a subtle point for my side. My cat and my
boy friend had not liked each other particularly. I
nudged the ring toward Shadrach, got up and made
myself a cup of tea. While the leaves steeped, I undressed, hearing small tinkles and metallic clunks
from the living room. But presenting the zircon to my
cat for a plaything was not the answer.

Artie was a heel and a coward, I decided fiercely—

and I was a stupid fool—but what when the crowd found out? I shivered with humiliation over the tea, but the only thing was to laugh it off, insist I'd never been serious, for heaven's sake. Artie was just a useful escort for as long as he was unattached, and I knew all about Poochy. I tried it, but I'm the world's worst liar. Everybody agreed: loudly, politely, over-heartily that of course it was only a gag. Nobody believed a word of it. For a week I was inundated with loving care, constant poppings-in to be sure I wasn't grieving alone. Karen conducted a nightly probe to be certain I was eating properly, and Rab made a wily request for a sleeping pill that was worthy of the Actors Studio! I almost hated to admit I'd never had a prescription; if I can't sleep, I take an aspirin. They were so obviously enjoying themselves taking care of Persis.

Nothing was seen or heard of the newlyweds; it was all dying down. And now that stupid Artie had to revive the whole thing, prancing into Trentini's as though all was peaches and cream. Didn't he know nobody liked Poochy in the first place? What in hell were they doing in the Village? Why weren't they living uptown in Poochy's apartment? Oh, heavens, she had a roommate, she must have moved in with Artie, right around the corner from me—I'd be falling over them every time I stepped out of my door—*oh, heavens!* The fight last night would be only the first of many. I'd have to apologize personally to Keoghan, who'd fed Shadrach twice a day for a week when I had a rush appendectomy.

I'd have to offer to pay for the damage at Trentini's, and I'd never dare show my face inside the door again. I said so, tearfully, to Marco.

"Tchk!" he twittered reproachfully. "It is not why I

call. Mama asks, please you will honor us for Sunday dinner?"

I said the honor was entirely mine, that I would arrive at seven—but replacing the receiver, I knew if Mama Trentini meant to defend me, I couldn't stand it. She had a heartful of love, a voice like a steam calliope, the memory of an elephant, and all the finesse of a bulldozer. No one would ever be allowed to forget that *povera bambina,* Persis Bradbury. I'd be hugged and kissed ebulliently, loudly commended for gallantry every time I smiled, constantly cited (in a raucous undertone) as a tragic example of incautious womanhood, and if I ever found another man (which isn't easy when you are six feet tall), I'd forever be assured, "Ah, you see? All ends for the best!"

I arose from my desk with decision and tapped on my boss's door. "If that job in Lisbon isn't filled, may I have it, please?"

Mr. Carvalhao's neatly waxed mustache twitched, like a pointer about to point. "Why?"

"A personal situation requires me to leave New York. It's either Lisbon, or resign and hole up in Texas on the pretext of settling Uncle Ted's affairs. Which?"

"Lisbon!" he said hastily. "After five years of training you to distinguish port from sherry, I can't afford to lose you now, Persis." I knew his sharp eyes had already noted the absence of zircon. He'd go home and tell Renée my engagement was broken and I was taking it hard, but so long as her adored Luis wasn't inconvenienced, she wouldn't give a damn. "An excellent plan," he was saying, enthusiastically. "You'll be there when we arrive for the mergers. I can easily make do with Miss Browning in the meantime, far better to have you in Lisbon, getting everything properly set up. Why didn't we think of this before?"

"Because we weren't thinking," I smiled at him with genuine fondness for his willingness to put up with a substitute at a moment's notice, no questions asked. "I'll be ready to leave Monday week, and once I'm over there, perhaps I can find a suitable girl to take over when the mergers are finished."

In twenty minutes the die was cast: Laura would sublet my apartment for six months, taking charge of Shadrach. "Of course I want him," she said indignantly. "He's exactly the arrogant touch I need." She wasn't fooled by my tale of crisis in Lisbon, though. "Yes, I know you always yearned to see Iberia," she agreed, "and of course it's more sensible for Carvalhao to send you to make things comfy-cosy before he gets there. All I say is, it's a highly opportune reward of virtue. Well, it's opportune for me, too—and we both know the condition of my virtue." She rang off, after saying I'd better pack away breakables, but needn't count the silver.

Between renewing my passport, sorting and packing, buying a few essentials for traveling, office 9 to 5 and impromptu bon voyage parties from 6 to 3 a.m., by the end of the week my major regret was leaving Shadrach. At least *he* didn't talk, although he was far from happy at the traveling cases and constantly underfoot. "No, you're not going, you're going to stay with Laura," I said firmly, dumping him into her arms, where he moaned wistfully—until she waved a small bag of shrimps under his nose, producing an instant growl of satisfaction. While he was occupied with shrimps, I got the bags and trunk closed, dispatched for cargo shipment, and gave Laura the extra keys. "I have to go, the boss said I could have an hour off, but I don't want to strain it," she hugged me tightly. "Have a ball for yourself, honey! Don't worry about a thing, I'll be back first thing after work to take care of Shadrach."

When she'd gone, I took a last walk around my home, holding Shadrach in my arms, and I suppose it was only weariness from the hectic pace of these last days, but I ended on the edge of the bed, bawling childishly. He purred frantically into my ear, until the bell rang, signaling the arrival of the car.

In it, to my discomfiture, was Renée Carvalhao, her dark monkey face peering at me sharply above the twelve-skin sable scarf she described as "utterly simply, but one needs *something* over a suit, after all."

In contrast to my old sealskin coat, my employer's wife was hard to take. I sank down untidily beside her, and she said, "Idlewild, Tompkins," with the same superb indifference to change that causes all true New Yorkers to refer, still, to Sixth Avenue. Before I could redistribute myself, we were off, and I was thrown painfully into a corner.

I made an effort. "How kind of you, Renée."

"Pas du tout," she grinned mockingly, drawing out cigarette case and lighter. "I wish to learn for myself of this sudden flight." She flicked the lighter expertly and ignored the sudden trembling of my fingers.

"Mama Trentini," I said, exhaling a cloud of her favorite Balkan Sobranies and suppressing the resultant cough—but there is one thing about Renée Carvalhao: unless Luis is concerned, she has instant grasp, total perspective, and one can tell her anything.

"You are well out of it," she stated at last. "A man who would buy a zircon for anything but an April Fool's joke—oh, *merde alors!* Such a man would not even have a dinner suit. Did he?"

"Well—no," I admitted, laughing helplessly.

"There you are, then," she said indolently and abandoned Artie to put on a pair of horn-rimmed spectacles and drag a wad of paper from her handbag. "I have written everything out for you. Stay at the Avis until you find a correct apartment, it must be on the heights with a view. For dinner, Tavares or Ramalhete, a private party, or Navigaciones. There must be a daily maid and a car." She peered over the notes. "You drive, of course?"

"Yes, but I can't afford—"

"Who expects you will?" she asked, surprised. "I pay any difference, Persis, although Sebastiao dos Martim can afford anything, I assure you." She snorted slightly at my blank face, and removed the glasses to stare at me impressively. "As well I came! You understand nothing. *Ma chère,* in Lisbon, you are not you; you represent Luis. His personal secretary expects the best, anything less is to insult Senhor Carvalhao. *Tu comprends?*"

She replaced the spectacles, riffling the papers. "Here are shopping addresses, local customs, people to know socially—I have already written them. If there is a difficulty, consult Rosa Limon; do not under any circumstances ask Luis's sister, she is a fool . . . but you are completely *comme il faut,* Persis. I have no fears."

Well, thank YOU, Mrs. Calabash, I said mentally, as we swung up to the airport. "Should I entertain?" I asked sweetly. "Two or four guests for a *recherché* evening?"

She was too absorbed in final reflections to get the point. "If you wish, *mignonne,* but do not exhaust yourself," she said absently, thrusting the papers into my hand. "Do not hesitate to telephone, even at day rates—but I have complete confidence in you," she smiled at me affectionately, while I was scrambling camel-fashion from the limousine. "You will be *épatante*—and Sebastiao is not there, after all, so you will be entirely safe."

I stood on the pavement and leaned to the window of the Rolls, while Tompkins trotted around to the driver's seat. "Why would I not be safe if Dom Sebastiao were in Lisbon?"

Renée looked up vaguely from the compact mirror in which she was critically studying the length of her mascaraed lashes, and recalled my presence. "Because he is a devil, and the whole family is accursed," she said, calmly. "Have a good trip, Persis."

The flight was smooth, the plane half-filled, and with no one in the seat next me, I had all too much leisure in which to consider the affair that was not an *affaire* with Artie. It was partly the reaction to sudden inaction after so much rushing about. I felt limp, bone-weary, wanting nothing more than to be home again, to bathe in my own tub with Shadrach sitting companionably on the loo cover, to turn out lights and fall into my own bed, to sleep and sleep, and wake to find none of this had ever happened.

"You are unwell, Miss Bradbury?" The stewardess leaned to me anxiously. "Can I get you something?"

I was conscious of tears dribbling over my cheeks, no wonder she was worried. "I'm—just homesick for my cat," I said, foolishly, hauling out a hanky and mopping my face.

"Ah," she sympathized. "Perhaps a drink?"

It sounded logical. I said I'd have Scotch; I think she brought me a double, but it worked. Slowly, perspective returned, together with inner honesty. *Face facts:* When you're a six-foot gawk in high heels (and why not wear them when you're still a giraffe in flats?), dates do not queue at your door. I did nicely through high school and college because everybody knew me, and I have the kind of family where something is always afoot. I was the kid sister, but even when my older brothers and sisters married, they only absorbed wives and husbands into the Bradbury fold, which continued to function as the sort of family to which outsiders felt honored to be invited.

So there were plenty of lads to call when I needed an escort, or to be sure of an invite to The Dance, and I wasn't thinking of marriage in those days. It was only when I decided to live in New York that I began to feel like a spinster. Mother looked dubious, tentatively suggested I'd be equally independent with an apartment in Boston, near my friends—but I had the promise of a job and I was looking for new worlds to conquer, so off I went.

I made friends, and there were men who repaid homecooking by theatre tickets or the newest nightclub—before marrying another girl. For a while it didn't matter. I was getting everywhere I wanted to go, seeing life in the big time and acquiring a formidable visiting list. When the fourth man married a half-pint who asked me to teach her how to cook, and the first man's wife tearfully besought me to baby-sit on a Friday because the agency had failed and Lew's boss was giving a party, I woke up. I agreed to baby-sit if I might bring my date, and by the faint silence before she said, "Of course, Persis," I knew she hadn't expected me to have a date.

On the promise of a good dinner, I bribed the man upstairs to accompany me. I had to listen to a very boring three-hour discourse on the general inefficiency and ineptitude of his co-workers at his even more boring job, but at least I had produced a man. When at last I got home, I undressed, fixed an unprecedented nightcap and settled to cogitation, with Shadrach curled in my lap. He was only a kitten at that point, but much as I loved him, I saw he was the ultimate symbol of spinsterhood. I ought to have bought a dog, except that I loathe them . . . but with a dog, I could prowl the streets legitimately, looking for men.

Instead, I'd instantly lost my heart to the black baby in the rear of the Chinese laundry. His mama and the rest of the litter were pure white, so he was obviously a badge of shame, and Mrs. Wing Looie was entirely happy to present him to me. "Mama not like, not feed good—you take, Miss Bladbully. Company for nights alone, velly intelligent, you see," she assured me happily. "Father in meat market, velly good cat, too."

It now occurred to me that Mrs. Wing Looie (mother of five with Number Six under her belt) had assessed me as forever unwed, hence in need of company. *And she was probably right,* I thought disconsolately. Without immodesty, I knew I had a literal host of friends: older and younger, married and single, spread all over the world, sincerely pleased to hear from Persis, always inviting me for dinner, a party, a weekend. People phoned from all over the country on the dollar rate, just to chat for three minutes. My mailbox was so full of foreign airmail flimsies, the postman had diffidently asked if he might have some of the stamps for his son's stamp collection.

Absently tickling Shadrach's chin, I thought, fairly speaking, I had a good life; it just wasn't good enough. All I had were friends; what I wanted was someone to love, some sort of home, a few babies.

That was when I got derailed. After a year of hunting about, Artie turned up.

Staring from the plane window, sipping my highball, I admitted to myself that at the age of twenty-six I'd been willing to settle for what I could get. My mistake was in thinking I could even get him.

It was a mistake he'd deliberately encouraged. I was still humiliated, wincing inwardly at the way I'd joyously latched onto him . . . introducing him to my friends, implying that we were a couple, publicly consulting him on whether or not "we" could do this or go there. Worst of all, when he'd produced the zircon (at dinner before the concert that happened to fall on my birthday), I had assumed it was intended for the special finger . . . *and he had let me,* when it would have been so easy to say, "Wear it on the right hand, hon—not good enough for the other."

Or something like that . . . Heaven knows he was facile with words!

How long had he been running around with Poochy on the side? We'd never been in each other's pockets, Artie and I . . . a daily phone call, dinner once or twice a week, the concerts, an occasional party or off-Broadway show. He had clients in show biz, to be worked with only in the evenings; I had my own friends. If we got back to the Village before midnight, we stuck our heads into our haunts until we found the crowd, and had a final beer together.

All very comfortable and informal for months—but now I realized several cogent points. He'd always known Poochy, of course—we all did, and didn't much like her—but Artie's interest in her had developed after he gave me the zircon. It was only in the last two months that I'd seen little of him. There were still the phone calls, the bi-weekly concerts, the appearance last thing at night . . . but there was also a new client requiring a special publicity campaign, tying up part of various weekends.

That was Point 1: he'd fallen for Poochy about six weeks, two months ago.

Point 2 was that, perhaps, he'd let me wear the zircon on the wrong finger because at that moment, when his affections were disengaged, he'd half-thought it might be a good idea to marry me since I so obviously wanted him. Poochy had swiftly changed that, leading to Point 3: she did it deliberately. In a way I couldn't blame her. She was a model, Artie was a top PR man, who could do more for her than he ever could for me. Except that she'd known he was considered my property, she'd ruthlessly set out to get him away from me. *Probably on her back*—I thought cynically . . . which was really Point 4.

Not in my tiddliest moments had I ever been tempted to bed down with Artie. I was entirely satisfied to have a man to hold my hand at the movies, put his arm around me comfortably while we were talking with the gang at Trentini's. I hadn't minded his kisses—they hadn't fluttered my pulse, either. It was simply status: a daily phone call, a man to cook for occasionally, a regular escort. But while Poochy was thinking they'd pulled the wool over my eyes, the truth was that I'd never suspected, because I didn't really care whether Artie was present or not!

Had I ever really meant to marry him? If he'd laid it on the line, said, "I've got the raise, let's get married?" would I have agreed?

At long last I was thinking, and I knew: in a year, I'd grown faintly bored with his classlessness. I *like* occasional evenings of formal clothes, expensive restaurants, taxis and orchids. I *like* an occasional reception with real caviar and foie gras, men with discreet decorations and conversation in four languages. I might never be able to convince anyone else, but I was glad he'd married Poochy!

I finished my drink, feeling cheerful. Too bad I hadn't handled it smoothly, but in six months I'd be a forgotten gossip item, and meantime I was going to a country I'd always wanted to see. A dinner tray slid before me. "Halfway there," the stewardess smiled. "Enjoy your dinner, Miss Bradbury."

It was somehow an omen that I should be looking forward exactly at the point of no return. Twenty-six isn't *old*, after all. Somewhere there was a man for me to lavish with true love, and when I found him, how happy I'd be to be free and available!

I picked up knife and fork, attacked my dinner and demolished it with relish, concentrating on the future that had finally arrived out of the past.

I was remembering Uncle Ted's reminiscent stories of people and places—gay, humorous, occasionally thrilling. He'd loved Spain and Portugal. "Happy people, terribly superstitious but friendly, and always game for adventure." So was Uncle Ted!

My godfather was daddy's half brother, born and

raised in Texas near the border, and a natural for a civil engineering job in Spanish Morocco. When it ended at the start of the Spanish Civil War, Uncle Ted turned into a sort of soldier of fortune: smuggling people plus valuables out of the country before Franco could lay hands on them. Much later, daddy told me with quiet professorial pride that there'd been an immense price on Uncle Ted's head!

I remembered him only vaguely . . . twelve years since I'd seen him last, when he came up to Salem from Texas for daddy's silver wedding anniversary. He was sporting a small mustache and mother trotted out every unattached suitable female for miles around. I don't know exactly what happened because I had to go to bed, but apparently she drew a blank all the way round, because Uncle Ted went back to Texas still a bachelor.

I thought now that it was tragic he should have survived Franco, and a tour with the Maquis when the second war started—to say nothing of mother's well-meant machinations—only to die of a broken neck, showing off at a local Texas rodeo.

Everything was left to me. "There'll be enough for college extras and a nest egg," daddy said gently, but at the age of sixteen I was inconsolable. "I'd rather have *him* than a nest egg!"

"So would I, but it's useless to rebel, darling."

I took a junior year in Geneva, I studied Spanish and Portuguese for Uncle Ted's sake, and for auld lang syne, Luis Carvalhao gave me a job in the stenographic pool—but I got to be his personal secretary on my own. I owned half a ranch in Texas—unfortunately not in the section likely to produce oil. Uncle Ted's partner was slowly buying me out. I'd made one trip to pack personal papers and what furniture would fit my apartment, told the man to use the ranch house as he pleased, and let it go at that. Readying the apartment for Laura, I'd impulsively stuck Uncle Ted's diaries into my travel bags; now was the moment to read them, when I was actually in the lands of which he wrote.

The stewardess was still keeping an eye on me. After a while, she slid into the next seat with cups of hot coffee, evidently determined to conquer my homesickness. Her name was Dorica Andreas, attractive though not exactly pretty. She'd been on the transatlantic run for five years. "You are traveling?"

"No, I'm going to a job in Lisbon for six months."

"Perhaps we shall meet again," she exclaimed cordially, giving me a visiting card. "That is my home; I come twice a week. Please, telephone if there is anything uncertain? My father is a doctor; my brother knows of lodgings."

"How kind of you! I want an apartment on the heights."

"Pedro will gladly help, and as soon as you have it, I will bring your cat. Oh, it's quite legal," she smiled, "but if I know, I smuggle him with me and talk to him, so he is happy."

"I never dreamed I could bring him. Oh, wonderful!"

"You have friends in Lisbon?"

"Only you," I smiled at her, "I'm supposed to stay at the Avis, but I expect Martim y Antobal will help me settle. I'm secretary to the New York partner."

"Martim y Antobal?" she echoed in a strangled voice.

"Yes. Do you know anything about them?"

"Only what all the world knows: he is rich and famous," she said after a moment. "Why ask me, Miss

Bradbury? I'm only an airline stewardess. If you will excuse me . . ." She got up abruptly and went away along the aisle, leaving me to drowse against the window. Fleetingly, I thought her reaction peculiar, but the firm was immensely old and influential. Perhaps it was rather like discovering she'd been trying to console the head secretary of AT&T or U.S. Steel.

I woke in the Avis at two, with sun thrusting inquisitively through the blinds and motor horns outside. Leaning against the window, I felt a surge of excitement. The final strain of landing, getting through customs and into a cab for the hotel, was done. I was *here,* and already I had a friend—although Dorica was formal and unsmiling as I came down the steps. "Thank you for flying with us, Miss Bradbury." After a glance at the gold-braided official next to her, I supposed convention was required. I might phone her this evening, say hello, suggest dinner or something.

Meanwhile, I decided on unexpectedness. Martim y Antobal should be demoralized by the arrival of Miss Bradbury on her very first day in Lisbon.

The building was old and staid, the reception room a slight concession to progress, furnished with a small brunette tittering on the phone. In a way this was homelike, but when her eyes ignored a visitor and her chair swiveled to continue the titters, I set a finger on the telephone button and cut her off. She swung around furiously, but I beat her to it. "There will be time enough for your business when you have attended to your employer's. Please tell Senhor da Velma that Miss Bradbury, who is secretary to Senhor Carvalhao, has arrived."

The poor kid nearly fainted! *"Sim, Sim,"* she whispered, frantically plugging and jerking buttons. "I do not know who is here—we did not expect—"

Eventually an elderly secretary was found, who looked perfectly distracted at sight of me, but by now I was enjoying myself. *"Faça favor,* I apologize for the inconvenient hour, but I wish to familiarize myself, so I shall not disturb anyone tomorrow."

"Sim, of course, but I am not perfectly certain . . . I am in accounting, you understand." She flustered forward, opening doors. "I believe Senhor Carvalhao occupies this room," she led me on to a dual secretarial office, "and one assumes his secretary sits here."

I stripped the cover from a rebuilt 1940 Royal Standard. "Arrange to replace this with an electric machine," I said sweetly, glancing into desk drawers, "and please have someone bring a full supply of paper, pencils, notebooks—everything. Tomorrow morning."

"Sim, sim," she agreed anxiously. "Anything else?"

"The location of the femina, where to hang my coat," I smiled. "Do sit down and have a cigarette, Senhorita . . . ?"

"Oliva—but we are not allowed to smoke in the offices."

"In that case, tell someone to bring me an ashtray—a *large* ashtray." I glanced about snootily. "I must say it's not what *I* am accustomed to. Who sits over there?"

"Senhora Dalmonte, secretary to Dom Sebastiao when he is here." Oliva's eyes glinted naughtily. "But of course he is so rarely here," she murmured, "and when he is away, there is little to do, *está entendido?* She will not return today."

"I see." In the space of a cigarette I'd picked her clean, and dismissed her, knowing by the click of her receding heels she was half-running in her eagerness to

recount the moment of glory. I lit another cigarette—
only four o'clock, might as well check Luis's desk, go
through his list of instructions.

The inner office was neat but dusty; was Dom Sebastiao's office equally untended when he was away?
I threw open blinds, and riffled through a formidable
pile of mail: three weeks' worth, or ever since the
bilingual had left. What was it doing *here,* in an unused
office? I found paper and pencils, went to work in
growing exasperation—because here were all the letters, forms, orders, confirmations, we'd been awaiting
in New York! Why had no one forwarded?

Finally I had a sizable package, but opening the hall
door I found only dark corridors and night lights. My
watch said 6:30. I went back to hunt for a mailing envelope. There were none in my desk. I tried Dalmonte's
and found them wadded into a bottom drawer that
stuck. I was struggling with it, when a deep voice
said, "Who are you and what are you doing in that
desk?"

"I'm Senhor Carvalhao's secretary, and I'm trying
to find a mailing envelope in this apology for an office,"
I snarled, "and if you're the night watchman, stay here
to let me out."

"It is forbidden that secretaries smoke," he said,
after a moment.

"So they said, and I'm not surprised. It's all of a
piece with the general inefficiency." With a final tug, I
released the drawer enough to drag out an envelope
and went back to Luis's office, telling the shadow in the
doorway, "Wait, if you please."

I packed up the papers, addressed the envelope, collected purse and gloves, turned off lights. The secretarial office was empty, but there were lights behind

the open door to the other executive office. *"Ça estou,"* I called.

A shadow approached the door and became a man whose head barely cleared the lintel. "So you are ready, Miss Persis Bradbury, but I am not," he said smoothly. "Your turn to wait, if you please." Backed by strong light from his office, he was overpowering: dark, erect, cavernous eyes and aquiline nose, faultless tailoring—and approximately six foot four.

"You're not the night watchman," I sighed resignedly.

"No—and then again, perhaps yes," he said, amused. "I am Dom Sebastiao Alessandro Duarte dos Martim y Antobal, at your service—although from your reaction to my establishment, it is no doubt you who will serve me. Come in, if you please."

Sinking silently into the chair he indicated, I had just enough spunk to refuse his proferred cigarette case. "A secretary does not smoke while in an executive office."

"Ah? There is more to this than I had realized. You shall tell me about it." He lit a cigarette for himself and turned to the papers on his desk, while I was kicking myself mentally. How could I have mistaken this man for a janitor? Even his shadow was authoritative! Well, if he fired me for impertinence, I'd enough cash to get back to New York. My watch said seven, my tummy said "When do we eat?" and he tossed the last paper into a file box.

"There," he said briskly, switching off the lamp and coming toward me, hand outstretched. Automatically I rose, and he took the envelope. "A major report so soon, Miss Bradbury?"

"It's not the outpourings of my maiden heart," I

said recklessly. "That's what someone *should* have been sending us."

He laughed heartily. "Oh, I see clearly I am in disgrace! Come, there is not a moment to lose: we shall post this, and you will outline my shortcomings at dinner."

"*Dinner?* It's very kind of you, Dom Sebastiao," I stammered in confusion, "but I'm not dressed . . ."

He shut the office door and looked me up and down deliberately. "On the contrary, you look charming, Miss Bradbury—and it is not in the least kind of me," he said calmly. "I detest eating alone."

The maitre d' settled us tenderly at a choice table overlooking the river, placed menus before us and departed. "You are amused, Miss Bradbury. May I share the joke?"

"Renée Carvalhao should see me now!" I chuckled, and relayed her impressive instructions, making a good story of it in response to the twinkle in his eyes—until the maitre d' returned in the nick of time to prevent repetition of that final remark. *He is a devil and the family is accursed, but you will be safe, he is not in Lisbon.*

Yet here he most assuredly was, ordering dinner across the table from me. I studied him with covert interest. I'd always chanced to be away on his rare visits to New York. The other girls were vehemently pro or con, from which I deduced he was a strong personality—but Luis was sincerely devoted to him, spoke of him with deep affection.

I knew a little, of course: he was forty-ish, a widower whose wife had died tragically. A son lived with Dom Sebastiao's mother, who was an Antobal and widowed.

There was a sister with some sort of eye trouble who was a friend of Renée. Mostly I knew the business: extensive properties in Brazil, wine export, a thriving sideline in cork products. Everything was coining money due to Dom Sebastiao's guiding hand. He was rich as bejasus, a birthright member of true international society, related to royalty and mentioned in the *Almanach de Gotha* as well as *Burke's Peerage*.

What *could* Renéc have meant? *Impossible* to think such a man threatened my virtue!

He'd dismissed the maitre d', sat back and smiled, "Now," he said easily, "we begin at the beginning. You are Luis's treasured secretary whom he kindly lends us to replace a girl who left at an awkward moment—which does not explain why you will stay for six months. Not that I shan't be *delighted* to have you," he inserted hastily. "Already I see you are what we have needed for a long time.

"On the other hand, in view of the speed with which you work—you arrive one morning, and by nightfall the deficiencies in my affairs are assessed, comprehended, and all is in hand—" he said admiringly. "I ask myself: what could possibly be in such desperate condition as to require six months of your expert supervision? Do you detect symptoms of incipient bankruptcy, Miss Bradbury?"

"Of course not!" In spite of myself, I giggled at his teasing grin. "I'm sorry I snapped at you, please forgive me? I was so *exasperated* to find everything simply sitting in an empty office."

"Naturally. I think you behaved with admirable restraint—and I still ask why you will stay six months?"

Well, I am the sort of person that, if you ask them a

question, they don't know any better than to answer it. "I'm supposed to be crossed in love," I said, as the waiter set a plate before me.

"And are you?"

I was inspecting the appetizer. "No, I'm well out of it," I said absently, "but my friends thought I was crushed and required consolation. What is this, please?"

"*Lagosta picante.* Tell me about this sad affair," he picked up his fork and neatly dissected his portion. It was a bit like lobster Cantonese, without rice and with cayenne.

"The only sad thing," I said frankly, "is that I made a blithering ass of myself, and now I'm thousands of miles from home and mother, to say nothing of my cat."

"Ah, a cat? Tell me . . ."

Shadrach lasted conversationally through broiled chicken and salad. "So you see I must find a home quickly," I finished earnestly, "because the stewardess will bring him at once."

"You would really feel at home," he nodded, and sat silently looking at the water while the table was cleared.

Reaction was setting in; despite the morning sleep, I wasn't adjusted to time change. If only I hadn't plunged down to the office, throwing my weight around, I'd never have met Dom Sebastiao, wouldn't be here making a fool of myself by babbling, boring him to tears, when he'd meant only to show courtesy to his friend's secretary.

"You are tired," the deep voice said sympathetically, "and I have only tired you further by making you entertain me. You have a gift for conversation, but it is unpardonable that I should make you amuse me only because I am bad-tempered. You forgive me?"

"Nothing to forgive," I stammered. "I'm sorry I talked so much, you can't be interested in Shadrach or my picayune love life."

"On the contrary," he said, slowly, "you're an extraordinarily stimulating young woman, and the man who fails to appreciate this is not worth your notice. We have spent," he glanced at his watch, "four hours together, and I assure you, if it were not that I know you're exhausted, I should not now tamely return you to your hotel!" He laughed softly. "No, indeed, I'm by no means through talking to you, but we will leave it for tomorrow night."

I stared at him uncertainly. What to say to this handsome fascinating suavity, who implied we would dine again tomorrow?

"Finish the coffee," he said gently, flicking a finger at the waiter. "You will sleep until you wake, *comprendido?* You will not present yourself at the office until after lunch," he tossed bills on the tray, pushed it aside and eyed me blandly, "by which moment all will be ready for your inspection."

"Oh, dear," I said sadly, "I'll never live it down, will I?"

"Nor I! Wait till you see the night watchman."

Moving through half-empty outer rooms, I said lightly, "Don't tell me: he's five foot two tall, five foot two at the waist, and a hundred and two next birthday! Oh," I stopped, raising my hand eagerly.

At a corner table was Dorica with a young man—or was it she? Out of uniform and in dim light, I wasn't sure. She raised her head, smiling pleasantly—then her face went blank.

"I'm sorry," I withdrew my hand, "I thought you were someone I knew. Forgive me for disturbing you."

"Por nada," she said politely, turning back to her escort.

"A friend?" Dom Sebastiao stood behind me.

"For a moment, I thought it was my flight stewardess," but as we were bowed impressively from the restaurant, I knew that girl *was* Dorica Andreas. I'd recognized the antique gold seal ring that was diamond-shaped rather than oval or circular. Why had she denied acquaintance?

Turning for another glance, I caught Dom Sebastiao's expression. There was no slightest doubt in my mind that he knew Dorica Andreas—or that she'd refused to recognize me because I was with him.

chapter 2

I didn't really think Dom Sebastiao would take me to dinner the next night, so naturally I wore my best office-to-date dress. In daylight, the mystery of Dorica seemed simple: they'd met on one of his plane trips, had a brief romance, and now wanted no reminders.

Was this what Renée had meant? So few girls are virgins these days, she'd assumed I wasn't, either? Sliding into the silk jacket, I thought that *if* I weren't, I'd fall like a Coney Island shooting gallery duck. But he'd done his duty by Luis's secretary, he wouldn't even be in the office today. Still, nothing could restrain my pulse as I walked into Martim y Antobal, to find expectancy in the air—for me.

I was awaited, fulsomely greeted, smilingly ushered to my desk, entreated to name anything—but *anything*—I desired. On one excuse or another, everyone from mail boy to spotty-faced file clerk came in for a good look at the American *secretária particular*. I got nothing done, of course, but there was an aura of heartening good will. I was still alone in the office; Senhora Dalmonte was at the warehouse. Dom Sebastiao's door was closed and presumably he was with her, at work. Well, I'd not really expected to see him ...

The hell I hadn't!

I slung my jacket over the chair, swiftly went through the mail, went to Files, which was deserted, and found my way to Accounting, which was half empty. "Coffee break?"

Senhorita Oliva shook her head. "We take turns for cigarettes in the femina."

I looked at two male clerks, cigarettes drooping from the corners of their mouths. "Who made this rule?"

"Senhor Valdes, the office manager."

"Does he smoke?"

"Sim—but his wife does not," she said, resignedly. Apparently nothing was more logical than an office force forbidden to smoke because the manager's wife did not! I went back to my desk, chuckling, and found a flashing light on Senhora Dalmonte's desk. Automatically I picked up her phone and pressed buttons without result. Behind me a door crashed open.

"I rang, Miss Bradbury. Do American secretaries ignore all summonses aside from their immediate superiors?"

"No," I returned, spiritedly, "but in America, lights indicate a phone; a buzzer is used to call the secretary."

"We wish you to feel at home; it will be installed tomorrow."

"Thank you." I picked up notebook and pencils with stern control. Damn the man, what was he doing here at nearly five o'clock, catching me off-guard again? "You wish to dictate, sir?"

He stood spread-eagled, braced against the doorjambs, his shoulders shaking with amusement. "The majesty of your stance, the disapproval in your blue eyes! What more have you to tell me, I wonder?" He laughed. "No, I do not wish to dictate, I wish to introduce you to your new home. Oh, the apartments I have inspected this afternoon!" He shuddered dramatically. "But I have found it!"

"I thought you were at the warehouse," I said involuntarily. Before the sudden gleam in his eyes, I could feel myself blushing, but he said only, "Shadrach requires an instant decision, but I shall be surprised if he does not find himself entirely satisfied. There are walls, flowers, several most respectable cats in the neighborhood."

Dom Sebastiao was rubbing his hands with glee, happy as a kid who just made the team. Had he really been apartment hunting? Absurd! He'd had the office call a rental agent and was now making a good story. Still, kind of him to take even that trouble. I thought warmly, he must be very fond of Luis.

He'd switched off lights, opened the corridor door, his eyes dancing with impatience. "Come, there is not a moment to lose."

I grew used to that concept, nor was it merely a joke— it equally well applied to business. Dom Sebastiao even drove his black Ghia with the same split-second decision; sometimes I thought perhaps that was what Renée'd meant, although he never had an accident. By the week's end I was breathless at the pace of life. It took him a single hour to evaluate my impressions, to initiate sweeping changes.

Now everyone smoked at her desk—with no excuse for gossip in the femina. Now there were buzzers, heard even when a back was turned at a file cabinet. When Senhor Valdes grasped this, I went to the head of the class; the girls were a bit disillusioned.

"Won't they ignore the phone lights now?"

"Never! The call might be for her."

Dom Sebastiao decreed I'd work on the mergers, Senhora Dalmonte would handle routine—a decision that pleased everyone. Elena Dalmonte confided she was not equipped, she worked only for the pension, *é coisa sabida?* "I was dreading, Mees! Never does he stay so constantly, it is exhausting merely to think—but now you are here, all will be well."

Yes, Dom Sebastiao was exhausting, yet exciting as a whirlwind. He'd taken me to Tavares after I'd taken the apartment. ("Come, there is not a moment to lose in obeying Renée's commands.") He'd ordered me to pack before coming to work, sent someone to pay hotel bill and transfer bags to apartment. "Renée advises a maid and a car?" Both were installed before I got to my new home. The maid was Teresa, the car was a Porsche painted sky blue. "It does not match your eyes quite so well as that zircon, perhaps, but at least there can be no doubt where you will wear it!"

Then, on Friday he was gone. "Always this way, Mees. He comes, he departs, who knows when he returns?" It didn't matter; I'd enough to keep me busy for days, plus a home to settle.

According to the map, Dorica lived only three streets away! An efficient voice said, "Doutor Silva's office, who is calling?"

"I wanted Senhorita Andreas," I said, "do I have the wrong number?"

"No, one moment, please." I sat, wondering whether Dorica were married, although she wore no wedding ring, and suddenly she was saying, "Hello?"

"Persis Bradbury," I said. "I've got an apartment, practically on your doorstep! 20 rua Pensilar—have you time to come see me?"

"Yes," she said slowly. "In about an hour?"

I told Teresa to make fresh coffee, and wrote letters home until the bell rang. Dorica looked white and strained, overtired from the last flight, but the friendliness was back. I led her from room to room. "Isn't it a dream! I can't wait for Shadrach, I've already written the friend who's keeping him. . . . Oh, Teresa, coffee on the terrace, please."

The maid took two steps and stopped dead, her hands trembling uncontrollably. *"Bom dia,* Teresa," Dorica said quietly. "A long while since we've seen each other. I hope you're well?"

"Sim, sim." Teresa hastily set down the tray and vanished, while I looked at my guest inquiringly.

She smiled faintly. "That's why I came. You've guessed there's a connection, a family matter," she said carefully, "only relating to the Spanish branch of the family, but the other night," she hesitated, "I thought— to know me *might* affect your job, although Dom Sebastiao only saw me once. Forgive me, Persis?"

"Of course—but he recognized you immediately, you know. Need it make any difference in our being friends, Dorica?"

"Would you dare?"

"I do not permit an employer to dictate except from nine to five," I told her, superbly arrogant—and it was true: Sebastiao dos Martim was not going to interfere. I felt strangely drawn to this girl, and I wasn't going to lose her. "How do you know Teresa, did she use to work for you?"

"She goes with this house. I lived here until grand-mother died, then I was sent to live with the Silvas," her lips twisted bitterly, "but one sees her in the street or at market, whenever Dom Sebastiao is expected." Catch-ing my wide-eyed astonishment, "This is the dos Martim town house," she said, surprised. "The lower floor, where grandmother lived, is for Dona Benedecta if she comes to Lisbon; above is for servants. It belongs to Dom Sebastiao, of course, but he only uses it . . ." She stopped short, flushing so deeply that I got it at once.

"You mean, I'm installed in his love nest?" One glance at her face was enough; I collapsed on the terrace lounge and shrieked with laughter. "Oh, and I thought you might be an ex-mistress, which was why you wouldn't recognize me. Forgive me, Dorica, but do admit it's hilarious! No wonder he could put his finger on the perfect place at a moment's notice, making a dramatic story of how he'd exhausted himself inspecting apartments for me. I didn't believe that, of course, but I did think he'd had someone telephone a real estate firm—and now it turns out he didn't even do that.

"Oh, when I think! I even haggled over the rent, until this oily creep . . . I wonder who he really was, because there wouldn't be any agent if Dom Sebastiao owns the house." I was gasping with amusement at the memory. "I said it was too much even for a short lease because I was only one person, and finally he said he was sure the owner would make a concession in view of my refer-ences . . . and all the time the 'owner' was standing right behind me, saying absolutely nothing."

Dorica looked faintly shocked as I sat up, wiping my eyes. "I wonder who had it last? Do you suppose she was dispossessed for me?"

She suddenly saw the humor of it. "If you really want

to know, I'll get it out of Teresa," she giggled. There's nothing like shared laughter to cement friendship. We sat limp, all barriers gone, chatting for an hour, until she said, "I must go, Persis. I'll bring Shadrach on the next flight—that is, if you want him so soon. Will you still be here?"

"Of course. Why not?"

"You're not afraid?"

"Of what? Surely you don't think Dom Sebastiao likely to attack me!" But she was unexpectedly sober-faced, even while she was shaking her head, and uneasily I recalled Renée's parting words.

"No, no, not that," she assured me. "He's a complete gentleman, never a breath of scandal. Oh, one hears now and then, or a particular name creates a discreet silence, *comprendido?*" She shrugged. "Why not? He's unmarried, after all. I don't know why he rented you the place, Persis, but you'll be entirely safe."

"Then what should I fear?"

"The Curse of Carranca."

I stared at her, bewildered, but it was beginning to make sense. *He is a devil, and the family is accursed.* Involuntarily, I gulped, feeling a faint chill running up my spine at her troubled face.

"I didn't know there was one." I made a try for normalcy. "You can't be serious? Oh, come now, how would it affect me?"

"I'm not sure it would," she said slowly. "All the same, there does seem to be something to it."

"Carranca . . . isn't that the family home?" I asked, vaguely. "Miles from Lisbon, isn't it?"

"Yes, the rest of the family lives there. I saw a picture of it once, and it's well named 'The Frowning House'—

but the curse is on the dos Martims. It has nothing to do with Casa Carranca."

"You mean, they carry it around with them like Typhoid Mary? What is it, exactly?" I was reluctantly impressed by her concern, on top of Renée's remark. If it were Dom Sebastiao himself who was supposed to be cursed, I could see it might appear to affect me—although aside from taking me to dinner twice and renting me his family home, I was no more connected with him than any other employee, and nobody in the office seemed at all worried.

"It grew out of a medieval feud. I don't know the details, but apparently the dos Martims cleared out the opposition by accusing them of heresy during the Inquisition, and the one who was burned at the stake is supposed to have cursed the dos Martims 'forever to lose what they love best in life.'

"I'm not superstitious, Persis, but you have only to read the history books," she said. "Century after century, from that time to this: tragedy, disaster, epilepsy, early deaths, even madness. Yes, I know you'll find much the same in lots of other old inbred aristocratic Spanish and Portuguese families, but by now—with modern medicine—most of it's gone. With the dos Martims—*it isn't*.

"Dom Sebastiao's wife fell downstairs and broke her neck; his sister Branca was an accomplished artist—she's nearly blind from some sort of accident. His mother, Dona Benedecta, was an international society figure; now she's crippled with arthritis, forever barred from the life she loved, I don't think she even comes to Lisbon any longer—and her husband, Dom Alessandro, was washed overboard years ago in a freak yachting accident. Not only the family, but sometimes people connected with them," she said in a low voice. "Two of the tenants here . . . one killed in an auto crash, the other in a skiing disaster.

"You see why I fear for you, Persis? Whether or not it's a curse or simply misfortune, whatever it is, it hasn't ended for the dos Martims with the discovery of penicillin and so on."

"It does sound grim," I said after a moment. "I never knew this before, but I can see how such persistent ill-luck would make almost anyone wonder if there wasn't something supernatural at work."

"Exactly! You're far too sensible to be scared by ghost stories, but I think you should know, so you can make up your own mind."

"Yes." I glanced about the pleasant terrace thoughtfully, glimpsed Teresa fussing in the kitchen, absorbed the mingled scent of roses and jasmine, the flowering fruit trees interspersed with green shrubs flung at random on the hillside below me. I thought of air-conditioning, modern plumbing, a reliable maid, a swanky car. Curse or no curse, I'd never find an apartment this good without indefatigable search—and when I turned up something reasonably approximate, it'd be twice (or more) what I was paying.

I said so, chuckling naughtily. "I wonder how much farther I could have beaten down the rent . . . because that's the answer, Dorica. I'm not his mistress, I never saw him in my life before that night at Navigaciones, and that was only because I'm his partner's secretary. I suppose he'd nothing else planned for that night, and he's very close to Mr. Carvalhao. He took me to dinner out of courtesy to Luis—but he put me here as the quickest way to get me settled, so I'd keep my mind on his business."

"I expect you're right," she murmured, but behind her smile I still sensed uneasiness. She got up, walking to the coping of the terrace. "I don't wonder you'd like to stay, the gardens are so lovely. Look, you can even see Doutor Silva's house." I went to stand beside her, following the direction of her finger. "There it is—the pink roof between the white and green tiles . . . See, that is my window to the right."

"Well, if we were teen-agers or Girl Scouts or something, and if we knew Morse Code, we could wigwag to each other after lights out!"

Dorica turned to me with a smile. "More or less what I had in mind," she said. "You see how close we are, Persis? So if you should be—uncertain, distressed about anything, you have only to walk down two streets and turn the corner. Already they know of you, want so much to meet you. Don't hesitate to call on them, day or night, even if I should be away." She looked at me compellingly.

Again I felt the *frisson* working up my backbone. "You don't really think . . ."

Dorica shrugged. "What's that quotation from Shakespeare . . . 'there are more things in heaven and earth.' No, I don't believe in curses, but I don't want to take any chances for you, Persis." She looked at me soberly. "It is strange," she remarked, "I do not make friends readily, for all it's part of my job to talk easily to strangers . . . but from the moment we met on the plane, I have felt a sort of kinship with you. I—somehow I couldn't bear for anything to happen to you. Please, you will go to Doutor Silva if anything disturbs you?"

"Yes, I promise—but it is strange, Dorica—I feel the same way about you!" I exclaimed. "I knew something was wrong that first night, but I was determined not to lose track of you . . . and the hell with Dom Sebastiao."

She smiled at me brilliantly. "That is so nice to hear," she said, "and I will bring Shadrach next trip, whether or no—because if anything changes, you will come to stay with me. There is plenty of space, and we are fond of cats!"

When finally she'd gone, I looked speculatively at Teresa, still bustling about in the kitchen—but one does not gossip about *autres temps, autres petites-amies.* I'd no doubt she knew every one of my employer's mistresses, and perhaps she'd let fall an unwary word if I were clever enough to get it out of her—but it was no concern of mine, and if Teresa suspected I were pumping her for sheer curiosity, she'd lose some of her respect for me.

I went back to the terrace and leaned over the coping, and as the twilight deepened, I could see a sudden light in the room Dorica had said was hers. Strange that she should feel as drawn to me as I'd felt drawn to her— but the light was somehow comforting.

I'd nearly finished the backlog; Dom Sebastiao was still absent. Senhor da Velma murmured "Oporto," which I gathered was practically unprecedented, when I casually relayed this to Elena Dalmonte. "How you know?" she breathed, wide-eyed.

"Senhor da Velma said so. Didn't you know where he was?"

She shook her head. "One never knows, until he is here." I wondered how on earth he made or kept appointments, but I couldn't have cared less where the man was at that point.

Daily I flitted down to the office in the Porsche, for which there was now a stall labeled "Mis Bratburry." It was next to that for Dom Sebastiao. Every time I parked my car, I snickered to myself, but I deliberately said nothing to anyone. I only wished I could be present when he first saw that sign. Nightly I flitted home again, to impeccable maid service and succulent meals.

On Thursday, Dorica called: "Shadrach is here!" An unmistakable feline howl was confirmation. Dorica laughed, "He objects to the carrier after sitting on laps all the way. We are four hours late, but Shadrach purred the nerves away. Captain Grandi does not wish to let him go, but here he is—and Pedro will deliver, I must get some sleep, but I see you tomorrow, Persis?"

"Dinner! Bring Pedro, if he likes to come," I rang off; one hour to clean my desk, I'd pull rank and leave early.

I parked the Porsche any old way at the curb, dashed upstairs to find Teresa beaming at the open door. *"El gato aqui!"*

It was a superb reunion, we kissed each other repeatedly, we talked back and forth while I changed into a housecoat. Never mind if we weren't talking the same language; we understood each other. He knew I was enchanted to see him; I knew he was enchanted to be here. He'd already eaten a dozen roses on the far wall and made a dirt wallow in the corner. I got my hairbrush and cleaned him up, while he purred ecstatically—and suddenly Teresa was fluttering at the terrace door with a tall figure behind her.

"Fique tranquilo, Teresa," Dom Sebastiao said easily. "I feel sure Miss Bradbury will not object to

receiving me, since she has no other guests."

"But I do—that is, he's a permanent guest," I said foolishly, because my pulse was throbbing oddly. "This is Shadrach, who just arrived, and we are making love to one another. Get down, Shadrach; this is Dom Sebastiao dos Martim." I struggled to get up, hampered by the housecoat, while Shadrach clung stubbornly.

"He is unimpressed, I fear."

"Shadrach, Dom Sebastiao pays the money that buys chicken wings!"

Instantly, my cat leaped to the terrazzo and walked across to gaze adoringly upward. Dom Sebastiao chuckled, reaching down to scoop him up. "Shadrach is a gourmet?" he asked, sinking into the other lounge.

"Naturally. Oh—won't you have a drink?"

"That would be pleasant, but do not disarrange yourself," he said casually, tickling Shadrach. "Teresa . . ." but already the tray was advancing, set beside him with the ease of habitude, while I stared at him. "Thank you," he said indolently, as she went away. With a final tickle, he set Shadrach on the tiles and said, "That is enough for a month of chicken wings; return to your mistress, if you please. Persis, I may fix you a drink?"

"Scotch and water, thank you. What a versatile man you are!" I was sweetly admiring. "One moment a landlord, the next—a bartender." He looked at me sharply, his hand suspended over the ice bucket. "I suppose I needn't tell Teresa you're staying for dinner, either," I observed, reflectively. "I don't know what's on the menu. Sorry . . ." Shadrach reestablished himself on my lap while I tranquilly sipped my drink.

"So you have been told something," he completed his own drink and straightened up. "I wonder what?" I stroked Shadrach and said nothing. "Or—by whom," he mused softly, his eyes on the cat. By a faint creak, I knew he'd sat down again.

"You are really angry with me," he remarked impersonally. "Why? Because I have rented you an apartment for which at the moment I have no use? Because I arrive without notice, merely because I am driving past, see a lighted window, and think I will stop to ask about the Merçadaria contract? I confess," his voice was humorous, "I hoped there might be a drink, but dinner was not taken for granted—although it is gracious of you to take pity on a tired man," he added politely, "and I accept with pleasure."

I couldn't rise to it, I was literally unable to open my mouth for fear I'd scream at him. I'd told Dorica it was hilarious—but was it? By what right did he walk in here, fixing drinks, using my first name, giving instructions to my maid?

"I must guess my transgression?" he asked after a moment. "Well, then—I deduce by Shadrach's presence that the stewardess brought him today, that her name is Dorica Andreas. She has enlisted your sympathy, and you have sworn undying friendship."

"We're friends, yes. She says there's a private family difficulty," I said steadily. "That's why she pretended not to know me, for fear it would jeopardize my job."

"And you told her your employer does not control your personal life," he finished smoothly, emptying his glass and smiling at me. "No more I do, aside from occupying as much of it as you permit. Continue, if you please." He reached a long arm to the tray and leisurely replenished his glass.

"Could we dispense with the honeyed words, Dom Sebastiao?"

"My friends call me Seb."

"But I'm an employee, though perhaps not quite the sort usually living here. I shouldn't like any misunderstanding on that."

He got up from the lounge with a rush and towered over me, his eyes blazing. "So that is what Miss Dorica insinuates? How dare she!"

"Perhaps because it was true of previous tenants, and she thought—in a friendly way—I ought to know," I told him with the calm of total recklessness, and got up to fix myself another drink, while he flung away to lean on the wall. "After the first moment of surprise, I thought it was the joke of the year for you to rent your *nid d'amour* to your partner's secretary—but I hadn't realized you went with the place as well as Teresa." I took a healthy gulp. "Whose was the Porsche, by the by?"

"Two or three back, I think her name was Inga." His glance was averted as he leaned among the roses, but I sensed amusement.

"Scandinavian? Ah, then I expect it matched her eyes?" My glance absorbed glass-topped dinner table laid for two, complete with candles and wine glasses.

"As a matter of fact," he ruminated, "I believe it was Lenore, after all. She had red hair . . ."

My fingers clenched on the highball glass. Teresa moved about the kitchen; Shadrach wreathed lovingly about her feet, and the twilight breeze held aromas of chicken mixed with roses. A pity to shatter the scene by hurling a glass. "Did she have her clothes made to match the car, or contrast?"

"I think she always wore white," he murmured dreamily. "Or was she the one who always wore black? Tchk, my memory is not what it was."

"As well; with all you have to remember, one would fear brain fever."

He threw himself around, clutching the wall and laughing uncontrollably, while I set down my glass carefully and turned to the door—to find Dom Sebastiao barring the way. "I will forgive myself for teasing you," he coaxed softly, "if you forgive yourself for goading me to it."

He set a finger under my chin and smiled at me. "My dear Persis, I've known for years that Luis and Renée are fond of you, at first meeting I know why. What more suitable than to settle you in our family home, where I know you'll be comfortable and safe in a strange city? But—American independence! I thought you might dislike to be lent an apartment, so I invent a story," he shrugged ruefully, "to be explained when Luis arrives. When I told him, he thought it a perfect solution."

"He *knows?*"

"Of course. He and Renée often stay here. Only this unlucky chance that you should meet Dorica Andreas! Heaven knows what she said, although I can guess from your reaction," he snorted.

"I didn't really think you meant . . ." I murmured miserably. "It was—the way you walked in, and Teresa not waiting for orders—but I *am* paying rent . . ."

"You'd every right to resent it," he agreed. "I was unpardonably thoughtless, but it was as I said: I was passing, it seemed natural to stop. There have, occasionally, been personal reasons," he said evenly, "but more often there are visiting friends. Tonight, I thought to take you to dinner and learn what has happened while I was away—and because Teresa is a family servant, she does not wait for your command. She is only a simple peasant mind."

"Yes. I've been shockingly rude," I said as steadily as I could. "I'm not able to forgive myself; could you do it for me?"

"Por nada!" He smiled kindly, looking over my shoulder. "Teresa says dinner is ready. Would you prefer to eat alone?"

"Of course not. How would I know which wine to open?"

He held my chair with a laugh. "You can't play ingenue with me, Persis; Luis told me long ago your palate is *formidable.*" He eyed me over the wine bottle, deliberately waiting.

"But never equal to yours—Seb."

He exhaled deeply. "Thank goodness! I may say I was dreading any more disapproval. I fear shortly the staff might have noticed."

"To say nothing of explaining to Luis and Renée!"

"Oh, nothing would be easier than to explain to them," Seb washed down a bit of roast chicken with a sip of wine. "The difficulty would be to achieve agreement on a viewpoint. Luis will instantly support my position; Renée, like all women, will instantly uphold rectitude . . ."

"Not," I said, "if Luis would be happier with depravity. If all I've got on my side is Renée, I'm licked before I start."

Seb choked slightly and laid down his salad fork. "One wonders whether your future husband will ever be able to drag himself from the fascination of your conversation long enough to consummate the marriage," he said helplessly. "Oh, *por deus,* Luis and *depravity?"*

"I expect he's a man like any other, if he gets a chance."

"Where did you learn so much about men, Persis?"

"Women are born knowing. For me, it's only academic so far, but I'm picking up tidbits here and there, to be ready . . ." I could feel myself blushing furiously at the revelation in my words, but Seb only said, "Tell me about your family, Persis. I think Luis said your father is a professor?"

We sat over coffee and liqueurs in soft night air with stars above, lights winking through the hillside shrubbery, and the scent of roses heavy in accumulating dew. Shadrach was chasing moths in the terrace lights. "They're a new and thrilling experience."

"When did he arrive?"

"Dorica brought him today," I said clearly. "She and Pedro are coming for dinner tomorrow."

Seb nodded. "Exactly what did she tell you, Persis?"

"Nothing vicious," I said after a moment, "only that there's a family difference, that she lived here once with her grandmother and Teresa worked for them—you own the building, this apartment was yours—but I couldn't see why I shouldn't stay, curse or no curse."

"So she told you!" His face was sardonic. "You are not afraid of curses?"

"As the descendant of a Salem witch, I'm not much impressed by other people's hexes," I strove for lightness, but he sat up on the lounge as though he'd just set a wet finger on an open wire.

"You are a *witch?*"

"No, of course not, it's only a family joke."

He stood up leisurely, extending cigarettes, lighting for both of us and sitting on the end of my lounge. "Tell me about this witch," he suggested, lazily.

"The first Persis Bradbury survived the Salem witch trials in 1692," I shrugged. "It's privately supposed the lad who tied her into the ducking stool made the knots a bit loose. Anyway, after three dunks, Persis was gone, and as only non-witches were supposed to sink, the township solemnly cleared her name and held a memorial service."

"How do you know she didn't drown?"

I chuckled. "She wrote her brother from Connecticut in 1682, commending her son to his care while at Harvard—and by a curious coincidence, her married name was Cornel, which was the name of the man who tied the knots."

Seb laughed. "So you are not really a descendant, it is only the name?"

"Oh, I'm direct. Around 1760, third or fourth cousins married each other, so Persis got back among the Bradburys, and I'm on that line—but if you're thinking I can do anything about your old curse, forget it," I advised. "I've got my own problems!"

His reaction was peculiar. Very slowly Seb's lips widened into a smile, until his shoulders quivered with silent amusement, and finally he stood up to throw back his head and roar with laughter. "Is this a private joke, or can anyone join?" I asked politely, but he only shook his head helplessly and refilled the liqueur glasses.

Still chuckling, he brought my glass and lifted his own dramatically. "A toast," he said deeply. "I will drink to your eyes, if you will drink to the only man in the world who has a witch for a secretary!" He tossed off the brandy at a gulp, and stood laughing at my bewildered face. "Bottom's up," he commanded, and when I'd choked down the brandy, he took both glasses and expertly shattered them into the trash can.

chapter 3

I told myself it was hero worship for a brilliant business executive; I knew it was love. Seb was in and out of Lisbon, always without warning. I lived for the days he was there, perfectly aware there was no future to this. In time I came to realize that Dom Sebastiao dos Martim was not only a tremendous bigwig in the Portuguese economy, but an immensely popular person in several strata of Lisbon society. No community endeavor, business committee, or swish party was complete without him, and for all this side of his life Elena Dalmonte was astoundingly efficient.

I listened with inner amazement to her suave telephone manners, observed her automatic handling of replies to formal invitations, ordering flowers dispatched to a hostess or sick friend. She never forgot a thing, never made a mistake.

When Seb appeared, Elena was ready with a report of his social and business schedule as of that moment, into which he could step for as long as he was in Lisbon. She had also a list of what he'd missed while absent, together with future dates that might be sufficiently important to bring him back on purpose to attend. Finally, there was a note of flowers sent, wedding or christening gifts she'd selected. I don't think he ever bought anything personally, nor even told her who or what, but her taste was excellent and her knowledge of subtle social gradations was unerring.

I viewed Elena with sincere respect. She might be unnerved by complicated business dictation, but as a social secretary she was superb. As she'd been with Seb for years, obviously he agreed. It was equally superb for me. I hadn't been meant to be more than the bilingual to take care of Mr. Carvalhao's requirements when he arrived, and when Seb calmly appropriated me for all the technical merger business, another executive secretary might easily have been miffed, leading to a chilly atmosphere that would inevitably have seeped through the whole office, with a taking of sides and general non-cooperation for the interloper.

Quite to the contrary, Elena was sincerely delighted to be relieved. Her pleasure was loudly expressed, she was as awed by my competence as I was at hers, and all of Martim y Antobal mentally genuflected to the excellent Mis Bratburry who was making life easier for everyone. Upon reflection, though, I chalked up another gold star for Seb. The Dalmonte might be perfect for his needs most of the time; he of all people couldn't fail to know she wasn't enthralled by his business, most of which she hadn't the brains to comprehend. She didn't even want to be in the know, she couldn't care less that someone else—anyone else—should be following the details of a most tremendous corporate coup.

She listened placidly to my bowdlerized version of daily decisions and accomplishments, and evidently passed along what she remembered to the Oliva and some other pals in the femina, but not so much for her status as to increase mine. She seemed sincerely devoted to Seb, yet with no particular emotion involved beyond respect and admiration, and I never saw him impatient with her when she had to ask him for a word she'd missed.

Where I was breathless at working with and for the keenest mind I'd ever encountered, could hardly wait for the next step, Elena only sighed, "Thank the good God you are here, Persis!" I wondered what on earth Seb would have done if I hadn't been there? I thought probably he'd have hired a battery of efficient stenogs and a translation service. Instead, he'd instantly latched onto me until Luis should arrive—and if he'd consulted Luis about the apartment, they'd probably agreed he should make full use of me. Clever Seb, to save the expense of half a dozen strangers poking about in his firm's business!

I didn't mind. At the end of two weeks, if you'd said, "Artie," I'd have said, "Who?" Life was more excitement than I'd ever dreamed. Everything was new and enchanting: delicious unfamiliar foods, sunshine and flowers, easy friendships, smiling neighborhood tradesmen waving jovially when I passed. Presumably Teresa had clarified my occupancy of the dos Martim apartment, for nowhere did I meet so much as a speculative glance.

At home I cuddled Shadrach and talked to him in English, so he wouldn't forget it. He was learning Portuguese too rapidly, due to kitchen chat with Teresa who was his slave, and had also made his way downstreet to butcher and fishmarket, where he instantly ingratiated himself. In fact, for a few days I was merely the owner of *el gato negro,* until they got the hang of my name.

Dorica came for dinner with Pedro Silva, who was evidently madly in love with her. He was interning, and there was no money at all. I was brash enough to ask, "Are you going to marry him?"

"Unless I find something better," she said blandly, and giggled at my expression. "No, not really that, Persis, but there is still almost two years before he can join his father. I do not think I shall find anyone I prefer, but Doutor Silva insists there shall be no formal engagement until Pedro is in practice.

"That is because of my job, and I suppose he is right. He almost always is. It's true that I meet men constantly. Perhaps there might be one who was irresistible. So far, not—but Doutor Silva says I must be free. We take betrothal very seriously here, you know, and if I were promised to Pedro, it would not be right for me to accept a dinner invitation from another man, even when I was alone in New York. As he says, I am young, I need some gaiety; it would not be good for me to be forced to spend my time only with other women or sit twiddling my thumbs until the return flight.

"On the whole it works very well. It is not easy for Pedro to wait and worry, but fortunately he is of an unusually sweet, intelligent nature." She smiled affectionately. "He knows I am not . . . rackety. Quite often there is a wife, or a daughter my age, and so long as Pedro knows, each time I return, that I still love him, he can enjoy hearing about life in New York. We have planned that that is where we will honeymoon."

Well, it did sound sensible. I thought she must really love him deeply to be able to wait two years. Via let-

ters, I introduced Dorica to my more blameless
friends, which produced a whole circle of respectably
marrieds for her to call and visit. Pedro was so delighted
that I'd more or less taken her out of circulation that
he asked me to the Interne's Ball. Dorica was en route
to New York, but as he was an inch shorter than I, she
had no fears!

Pedro and Dorica were my closest friends in Lisbon.
We were oddly like a family, with no hesitation about
phoning at all hours, making or breaking engagements.
Doutor Silva and his wife treated me like an extra
daughter, which was enormously comfortable. If Dorica
were away, and Pedro off duty, he'd drop by for a cup
of coffee on the terrace. He spent most of the time
talking about Dorica, but I thought it was all going
to work out magnificently. He hoped eventually to
specialize in surgery, for which his professors said he
had a talent. "I am luckier than almost everyone!" he
said. "Once finished, my father will make room for me
in his practice. Can you think what that means?" he
asked earnestly. "True, I must build my own practice,
but to have the office, the patients, the sponsorship!
My father is highly respected; merely to be his son guar-
antees I can build a practice as quickly as I can prove
myself . . . so almost at once, I shall have something
to offer Dorica."

"You'll get married right away!"

He shook his head. "Automatically she loses her
job when she marries, and I shall not have enough
money at first, but at least we can be betrothed."

"Nonsense!" I was forthrightly American. "She'll be
worth a packet to any local travel agency. Get married
at once; you've waited long enough. By the time she's

pregnant, you'll be established a bit, and she'll have earned enough money to cushion things."

He laughed helplessly. "You are entirely practical, Persis!"

I had other friends in Lisbon. Elena Dalmonte tentatively invited me to dinner, and apparently I made a good enough impression on her husband and children that the Oliva timidly suggested dinner with her family. The unexpected meeting of minds was Senhora Valdes. She didn't smoke because she was a singer, and what a lovely voice she had! Through Juana Valdes, I met the Lisbon counterpart of Greenwich Village.

Even more unexpected, I was instantly accepted and welcomed with open arms—because I was Dom Sebastiao's secretary! The mere name was a passport to every atelier, every tiny gallery, music or dance studio, *boite* or coffee house in town. "But yes, he is a patron, *comprendido?* His taste is superb, if Dom Sebastiao buys a painting or sponsors a showing, one is truly encouraged, one knows his work is good, one has the heart to try twice as hard. It was he who paid for the recordings of Simon, that led to an appearance on American television; one hears now that Simon is famous, goes to Hollywood for a film! Oh yes, we know Dom Sebastiao well, one night you will see him at that corner table, enjoying the dancing with a snifter of brandy . . . see, this is the glass he brought us that we keep for him . . ."

It was a facet of Seb that was almost more intriguing than the social lion, the aristocrat, the business executive, and all part of waking eager for each new day. Uncle Ted had said the Portuguese were friendly; indeed they were. They not only liked me, they liked my friends when I mixed them all together. Now I could introduce Dorica to Juana Valdes, go unescorted to Pernota or Figaro to hear the latest sensational guitar, take the Oliva to an atelier party that gave her a heady taste of Life. I wrote voluminous rhapsodic letters home, arranged for Dorica to spend a weekend in Salem with my family; I bought a small view of Setubal from one of the aspiring artists, and posed with Shadrach on the terrace for two others who were enamored of my blonde hair and black cat. I drove to Sintra, swam at Belem, dined at Alcantara, picnicked at Sezimbrá and water-skied from Seixal.

Pleasant as it was, as the weeks rolled by I was increasingly aware of a certain dichotomy. Sitting at my desk, transcribing notes, watching the mergers grow under my fingers, I was wholly absorbed by Seb's business and his expert flair in the handling of it. Over the typewriter, I merely admired the brain. While my pencil flew over the shorthand notebook, I was concentrated on getting every word, doing the best possible job to match his, and knowing I was turning out exactly what he wanted.

He never praised. I understood that, too. During business hours, Seb was wholly concerned with his work, yet the mere expectation that whatever I handed to him would be perfect was flattery enough. He gave me no directions beyond which transcription would be needed first. After a while he did not even tell me that: it was even more flattering that he assumed I was smart enough to know. The pace became frenetic, as drafts were revised to be typed with legal precision—meaning no erasures. Once he said, "It will be too big a load for you to handle alone, Persis. Get a legal secretary to do the finals. We're falling behind, and I need you for dictation."

"Do it the other way round," I countered. "Dictate to a tape recorder; let Elena transcribe for a draft. I'll do the final. We'll only waste time breaking in a new girl."

He nodded briskly. "Good idea. Take care of it, please."

I got a battery of machines: one for his office for the dictation, one for Elena for transcription, and a battery operated job to carry with him when traveling. "You might have time to make notes or dictate routine correspondence . . . and I got all three speeds for Elena's machine, so the reels are interchangeable."

He eyed the recorder inscrutably. "How does it work?" I showed him. "Watch the volume, your voice will boom if you're too close to the mike . . . There's a signal light on the office machine, but with the small one, you'd better practice a bit to know where to hold the mike, or it'll break Dalmonte's eardrums."

I'd expected a major snow job to convince Elena, but amazingly, she took to it like a duck to water! *"Sim, sim,* you are quite right, it is easy," she said enthusiastically, "but anything is easier than taking Dom Sebastiao's dictation in person! Now it is possible to turn off the machine when one wishes to sneeze, which is not possible when one sits beside a desk, *é coisa sabida?* One cannot turn off Dom Sebastiao, after all."

No more one could . . . and the relationship between us was peculiar indeed. When business was over, I could let myself realize I loved this man. The supple movements of his fingers curling about a cigarette, the curve of lips when he smiled, the flashing dark eyes twinkling with humor, the lazy deep voice, the warm hand cupped about my elbow to assist me into a car or out of a restaurant—because over these weeks we were growing closer and closer.

Seb would whirl into the office, summon me and dictate briskly for an hour or go over the material I had ready for him. Then he'd say, "Transcribe tomorrow, Persis. Let's have dinner. Are you free?"

Once I had to say, "I'm so sorry, I'm meeting friends at Aquario."

"Ah?" He stood up, stretching lazily and smiling at me. "Another night, then. Order the lobster gratinée, you will enjoy it."

I ordered the lobster, I did not enjoy it. I could scarcely keep my mind on the conversation, could hardly wait for the whole evening to be ended. That was the night I sat on the silent terrace, anguished, knowing that if Seb were not a gentleman, if he said the Portuguese equivalent of "How's about it?" I'd say, *"Sim, sim!"*

It would never happen, of course. He had no thought of me beyond the companionship in the office that extended into dinner because I was an American business woman and his partner's secretary, and I would not misunderstand such an invitation. He was fifteen years older and wiser than I, he knew the world, including the social freedom of American girls.

So it meant nothing that he should take me to dinner when he'd never similarly honored the Dalmonte, nor any other employee. The whole office took it in stride: it was perfectly all right for Dom Sebastiao to invite Mis Bratburry to dinner, very publicly in the most exclusive expensive restaurants, because she was American, and one hears such things are *hokay* over there, while for a Portuguese gentlewoman—even of uncertain age—it would be an evidence, a distinguishing attention, *é coisa sabida?*

Martim y Antobal actually felt even more warmly toward Mis Bratburry, for it was well known the boss was a solitary man, and right at this moment, with so much on his mind, to whom could he talk so freely? Further, I gathered by an unguarded word from Elena that he was between mistresses at the moment. How fortunate that there should be available a suitable young woman to be company, help him to relax! I wasn't sure whether or not to be flattered that the staff was so convinced of my virtue, but of course if they'd taken it differently, Seb would have stopped asking me. He would never have embarrassed Luis by giving me a questionable reputation in Lisbon.

Between my own firm commonsense and the office reaction, I took everything at surface value. It was partly that he detested eating alone, and partly that he could talk freely to me. Like any secretary, I always had a piece of paper and a pencil with me; once in a while, Seb had a bright idea at the dinner table, and I'd say, "Hold it until I get the book!" I didn't care what his reasons were, so long as I could be with him for an extra hour or two. I didn't even worry over an eventual broken heart, because I expected nothing. Nothing was possible to expect. I was quite resigned to my fool's paradise, but still determined to get every jot or tittle available.

After the Aquario tragedy, I became evasive about positive engagements. I couldn't bear the thought Seb might arrive again, late in the afternoon, to say, "Are you free, shall we dine together, Persis?" Via Elena's "important" list, I could generally guess when Seb would not ask, when he'd be in Lisbon primarily to attend a business dinner or special social event. Even so, he crossed me up once or twice when I knew he was expected at a private party . . . but I thought he was probably too tired for politeness, and it was apparently accepted in Lisbon society that one only asked Dom Sebastiao, and expected him when he arrived.

This particular night, by great good luck, I'd meant only to eat at home and see if Pedro would like to go to Pernota's later. Seb's face was lined with strain, tense after the long drive down from Oporto. "Why not come to my place?" I suggested, impulsively. "I'll call Teresa."

He grinned at me ruefully. "Oh, I always forget the American generosity! I'm caught, I must confess—I have already called her," he deposited a light formal kiss on my hand, "because it is only the American woman who really knows how to spoil a tired man. You will forgive me?"

"Of course."

I'd have forgiven him anything and everything, not that it was necessary. Presumably he had an owner's key; he always rang the bell. After that first night, he always asked permission to fix drinks, or to sit on the lounge. The instant Seb was settled, Shadrach leapt into his lap and purred man-talk until Seb would say, "Enough! You have convinced me I must pay for chicken wings next week, but now I wish to talk to your mistress."

Actually, he talked very little; it was I who babbled along, because he was forever asking questions, and as I said before, if you ask me, I answer. This can easily take anything up to an hour, depending on what you asked, but Seb stayed with it, no matter where I wound up. He never forgot anything, either. He knew the names of my two sisters and brothers, their families, where they lived, how old the children were, and the results of their last toothpaste tests.

He never spoke of his own family. When I asked about his son, he said, "Duarte is ten, he lives at Carranca with my sister. He should go away to school next fall. I'd thought of sending him to Eton, but now I'm wondering whether an American school might not be better. What do you think, Persis?"

"I don't know," I said dubiously. "Our schools are terribly crowded with the population explosion, you know. While you people were fighting over here, apparently we were breeding like rabbits. I can write daddy and see what he thinks."

"Would you do that, Persis?" He smiled appreciatively. "I hear you bought a painting from Lora— may I see it?"

"Of course . . ." but somehow we never got back to Duarte.

Seb was utterly comfortable to be with; I could say anything or everything, and he'd be with it at once. I let him set the course of the evening. Sometimes he took me out to dine, sometimes we ate on my terrace that was really his—although I paid my rent *on the dot,* very deliberately and wondering what in hell he did with it.

He looked at the painting I'd bought, and said, "You have good taste, Persis. How much did you give for it?"

"Fifty dollars, which is twice too much at the moment, but he needed a bit extra for the new baby, and I happened to have it," I shrugged casually. "And of course it'll be worth five times as much in five years. Don't you agree?"

Seb's eyes were sharp. "You knew I had bought from Lora?"

"No—although I couldn't imagine you'd have overlooked him, but he didn't say so." I stretched lazily, contemplating the picture. "How many do you have?"

"Ten—no, eleven," he said after a moment. "You consider them a wise investment?"

"Oh, definitely!" I assured him cordially. "When I get home, I'll show this to Perls or Knoedler. I miss my guess if they don't hot-foot it over here on the next plane. Paris is finished for new artists, these days. One can do better on the left bank of the Hudson."

"You know these dealers personally?"

"No, but if Lora's as good as I think he is, I'll have only to walk in and show that picture. It's not for sale, so whoever's the top banana will be willing to look."

He chuckled. "So you will create a market for my investment?" But neither then nor later did Seb ever express any comment on my critical tastes. I didn't care; I knew Lora was a comer . . . which was more than could be said for the two lads who'd painted me with Shadrach. *"Por deus,* what were you about, Persis!" Seb snorted, when the two canvasses were standing in a corner of the terrace.

"Yes, they are rather dreadful, aren't they?" I agreed, looking at myself with three eyes on one side of my nose. "But if Felipe could be persuaded to be himself instead of a road company Picasso . . . and Jorge could be lured into trying commercial art, I think they might both make a satisfactory living, don't you?"

"Perhaps. Do you think you can do it?"

"I can try."

"How much did you give for these—monstrosities?"

"Six good dinners," I said sweetly. "Will you fix me a drink, please?"

Mysteriously there was always enough for two, even if I didn't telephone Teresa, but I no longer cared that she set him above me in importance. I did, too. Coquetry is not for me. I was born to wear my heart on my sleeve, to be humbly grateful for a crumb of flattery, a hundred percent faithful at forsaking all others. Not too difficult. Few men make passes at six foot lasses.

Still, I was not languishing nor unhappy during those weeks. I was quite adjusted to the thought that Seb was not for me, but even though it would be devastating when I had to go back to New York, the mere fact that there existed in the world one very tall, intelligent man guaranteed there were others, as nobody but an Einstein is unique.

I was not thinking in terms of Dom Sebastiao himself, but somehow entirely content to love him *pro tem*, as an encouraging symbol of better things to come for Persis Bradbury. He never looked a look, nor said a word, never touched me beyond the most conventional arm down a stairway or across a street. Without immodesty, I knew he enjoyed dining with me. I was content to be a junior grade Scheherazade storing up anecdotes, office gossip, to amuse him—quite satisfied if I could see him relaxing, leaning back in his chair, chuckling casually.

On a Thursday I called Dorica at two minutes to five, intending to say, "I'm free, have dinner with me

and let's go to Figaro later? My party" (that was because Pedro had so little money, but I'd got him convinced this was the way American women did things!)
"and there's a new singer Gusto thinks we'll enjoy . . ."

That's what I'd meant to say, but the door opened
and Seb went through like a tornado as usual. I
switched rapidly to, "I can't make it, the place is a mad-
house, and he's just buzzed."

"I'm sorry to miss you, better luck next time." Her
voice bubbled with suppressed amusement. "Enjoy the
dinner, Persis."

I hung up sadly. Had I been seen somewhere after
breaking a date with Dorica, or was I simply transparent? Perhaps it was only because she had her own
love that she understood mine.

It was not all a lie. Elena tottered distractedly from
Seb's office, hissing, "He wants you." When I went in,
he was bent over a drift of papers, scanning, discard-
ing, making notes. I stood silently waiting until he
looked up and said, impersonally, "Do you have an
evening dress with you, Persis?"

"Yes."

"I should like you to attend the Commerce Club
banquet with me tonight. Be ready at seven, if you
please." He went back to his papers, and I went back
to my desk—but with a glance at the time, I packed
up and left. If I were to represent Martim y Antobal
at a formal party, preparation was required.

Surprisingly, Teresa was an excellent ladies' maid!
When I flew into the apartment, breathlessly hauling
out my one evening dress, explaining why it was needed,
Teresa simply took over! The dress was faultlessly
pressed by the time I crawled out of the shower. All
accompaniments of underwear, hose, shoes, were wait-

ing—as well as Teresa. Ruthlessly, she pushed me into a chair and toweled my damp hair, deftly combed and pushed it into a few deep waves, a row of end curls. "To the terrace, in the sun," she commanded, tugging a chair into the last rays of light, and settling beside me with a bowl of warm water. "The right hand," she said, and proceeded to give me a most efficient manicure!

If this was the service that Seb's mistresses received, I could envy them for more than merely a shared bed! By the time Teresa was finished with me, I was garbed, coiffed à la Kenneth, and was adding discreet dabs of perfume and my few bits and pieces of jewelry, which consisted of a modest string of amethyst quartz with a carved pendant to blend with the violet chiffon of my dress, and some dangly Greenwich Village amethyst earrings. Teresa had gone away to answer Seb's ring, and presumably shown him to the terrace, while I collected evening purse and the embroidered shawl I used for an evening wrap. I found a pair of white gloves, transferred keys and a hanky to the purse with enough change for the femina . . . and looked at myself in the long dressing mirror.

I was suddenly uncertain. This was as good as I'd ever look, I knew that, but it was no approximation of what Sebastiao dos Martim was used to in the women he escorted, I knew that too. How could I do him credit in a five-year-old dress, costume jewelry and the Spanish shawl I'd found among Uncle Ted's possessions? I might love it, the embroidery was exquisite, but already there were a couple of tiny slits in the silk . . .

Teresa returned. "Dom Sebastiao waits," she said, and stood still, staring at me in smiling admiration.

"Eh, you are very beautiful tonight, Mees! Turn about, *faça favor . . . sim, sim,* all is perfect except for the shawl . . . it should be worn thus, and you will hold it with the other hand, *comprendido?*" Swiftly, she'd rearranged it, murmuring to herself "Ah, it is very old, and very lovely! How fortunate you are to have it! Now, the flowers . . ." She produced a small corsage of fragrant valley lilies and white camellias, and stepped back, debating, her head cocked to one side. "On the wrist," she decided, and quickly tied them in place. "Now, you are ready. Enjoy yourself!"

Teresa's approval bolstered me a bit. She must have seen many a girl going out with Dom Sebastiao from this apartment; if she saw nothing wrong with my appearance, perhaps I'd get by. I was still timid when I went out to the terrace, where Seb was lounging over a drink and chatting with Shadrach. "Did I keep you waiting? I'm sorry."

For a moment he held his glass suspended, looking at me. Then, he'd uncurled himself, gotten up in one lithe movement, still holding Shadrach in one arm. "My dear Persis, you are a model of punctuality among women . . . fifteen minutes? This is some sort of record, certainly! But if it were four times as long, you would be worth waiting for, eh, Shadrach?"

In the gathering darkness I couldn't see his face, but the voice was lightly humorous as always. With one arm he released Shadrach to leap down and come toward me . . . with the other he finished his drink and set aside the glass. "I am impolite to enjoy a drink, and refuse you the same . . . but you shall have a double when we arrive."

"Oh, dear," I said despairingly, "have you been cuddling Shadrach all this time? We can't go until you're brushed, he's shedding like mad . . . Teresa, find the clothes brush, please?"

"*Sim, sim.*" She scuttled away, came back while I turned on the terrace floodlights, and Seb looked down at his clothes aghast. "*Por deus,* I never thought . . ."

"No, I know you didn't, and you couldn't see in the darkness." I took the brush from Teresa and went over Seb's coat efficiently, but there was still a drift of hairs. I ruffed the brush and poked it at Teresa. "You go on brushing, while I find the scotch tape, and if we're later than late, don't complain," I said crossly. "Anyone knows better than to make love to a cat in springtime, particularly if you're wearing evening clothes!"

Between us, Teresa and I got him cleaned up, de-haired and ready to go in another fifteen minutes, while Shadrach sat on one of the terrace tables and observed our efforts with interest. Seb was equally interested. "What are you doing with the scotch tape?"

"Blotting up the wisps, of course." I'd used half the roll before I'd got the last hairs. "There. You'll pass muster—but for heavens' sake don't ever pet cats or dogs again when you're wearing evening clothes. Turn around . . . slowly . . . Teresa, is he all right?"

Obediently, Seb revolved, stiff and poker-faced until he was turning back to us—when he pretended to be a lighthouse, grinning widely as he went around into darkness again. Even Teresa tittered faintly, while I was helpless with laughter—but it had taken me out of my uncertainty, and restored perspective. I was only a secretary, after all; Dom Sebastiao could never have expected me to possess an elegant gown or real jewelry. What I had was both becoming and suitable, Teresa had added a bit of gloss, and here I was: off to the ball.

The instant Sebastiao appeared, he was surrounded, almost overwhelmed by eager greetings that flowed over me in a backwash of cordiality. All Lisbon was delighted to make the acquaintance of Miss Bradbury who was Luis Carvalhao's secretary in New York, but it was Seb they mostly wanted to see. "Where have you been? No one has seen you in weeks! Rosa was *devastated* you failed her dinner party . . ."

"I was desolated to miss it, but when one travels . . ." he shrugged, half-turned to twitch a wicked eyebrow. I barely stifled a giggle, because that very night Seb had been stretched on my lounge chair, replete with Teresa's *bacalhao* . . .

As banquets go, it was a banquet; no more need be said. The food was a bit better than at similar affairs in New York, the speeches a bit shorter. Seb gave a brief report on the status of some local legislation the group was sponsoring. The dinner tables were rapidly removed, the dinner music combo augmented for dancing. Everyone did his duty by Seb's guest, so I was looking down on bald spots as usual . . . until the orchestra swung into a Viennese waltz and Seb bowed formally. "Do you reverse, Miss Bradbury?"

"Constantly," I assured him, and with a laugh he put his arm about me and whirled onto the floor.

Only a beanpole knows the joy of a tall partner! Seb's rhythm was faultless, our steps matched perfectly, until we were moving as one. It was like flying, weightless somersaults in space, heaven. For a moment he held me as the music ended. "We've done our duty; shall we go, or stay to dance again?"

An insistent little man tugged at Seb's elbow. *"Faça favor,* we exchange the next dance, Sebastiao?"

Another bald spot—after Seb? "I'm a little tired, would it be all right to leave?"

"*Por deus,* I wish we'd never come, except for this dance . . ."

"It is not a conventional hour, but there is a matter of business. Will you give me a cup of coffee?"

"Of course."

"It is that I must go to Brazil next week," he said, carrying his cup and rambling about the silent terrace. "I should like you to come with me, Persis."

"Well, if you need me, of course—but surely they've a bilingual?" I said, startled. "It's awfully short notice, I don't know if my passport's valid for Brazil. When would I have to be ready, how long will you want me?"

He set the cup on the table with a thump and turned to me. "Always," he said in a low voice. He drew himself erect, the lace ruffles of his evening shirt catching the terrace lamplight like a row of butterflies. "Persis—*queridinho*—will you do me the honor of becoming my wife?"

There was an agonizing silence while I tried to find my voice. "*Me?*"

"You," he said softly. "You—and no other. Will you marry me, my blue-eyed witch?"

"Yes," I said numbly, "but—why me? Are you sure?"

"Absolutely!" he chuckled, "and if I'd had any doubts, this proposal would have settled them!" In two steps he'd pulled me into his arms, laughing exultantly. "Why? Let's say it's because I can kiss you without a crick in the neck!" He laughed again, and proved his point.

*   *   *

I went through the next days in a trance. We telephoned my parents; Seb formally presented credentials and requested daddy's permission to marry me. By the time I got on the phone, daddy was sounding bewildered, but game. Mother was less easy. "Persis, are you sure? So much older, and a widower, all so sudden—can't you wait a bit?"

"No, I can't, mother. I want this one."

"All right, I'll send you the family veil," she stated. "There'll just be time—and there's no luck without it."

I told Teresa I'd be away on a special assignment. Shadrach would be unbearably spoiled, I knew. In the old days, travel bags were greeted with howls of despair and attempts to secrete himself among the underwear. Now, he simply made sure Teresa wasn't packing, too, and purred companionably while I filled the cases.

We were married in the American Embassy. I wore a white silk suit and the Bradbury veil. The Ambassador's daughter was bridesmaid, and a quiet smiling Englishman who'd been at school with Seb had flown down to be best man. There was a glass of champagne all round, a babble of good wishes, hearty hugs and kisses. Then we were at the airport, with Seb shaking hands. "Thank you for coming, Charles."

"Wouldn't be legal without me! Must say you've done well for yourself this time, old boy!" Charles kissed me shyly on both cheeks. "May you be happy forever, my dear Persis!" In the general dreamlike quality of the day, I was too warmed by his sincerity to grasp the wording until much later—when all that assured me of reality was the intricately wrought gold ring on my left hand and the hum of airplane motors.

"Who is Charles?"

"Viscount Mallory, my fag at Eton. He liked you; did you like him?"

"Very much. He said 'this time'—is he your permanent groom's man?"

Seb's face went blank. "Does it bother you that I've been married before?" he asked obliquely.

"I hadn't thought," I said uncertainly. "Isn't it the other way round, really? You know how to be married and I don't, yet. You'll have to tell me things and put up with me—but I'm very teachable," I finished hopefully, "so if you'll just remember I'm doing my best, we'll see where we wind up."

The dark eyes were expressionless. "Why do you mistrust yourself? Did that—sad affair in New York mean so much as to kill your self-confidence?" he murmured. "Persis, *querida,* your best will be all—perhaps more—than I need!" He laughed softly, patting my hand, but again I had the impression of a private joke.

"What is this envelope that comes between us when I wish to hold your hand?"

"The Bradbury veil. I want to return it at once, before anything happens to it—so sweet of mother to send."

Seb nodded. "It beautified you," he said impersonally. "You were—electrifying, *minha amor.* Did you regret marrying so far from home and family?"

"Yes and no. I never visualized floating up an aisle with eight bridesmaids. I'd have looked like an ocean liner being berthed by a flock of tugs," I remarked. "Nice if my parents had been here, but not an emotional necessity—and there wasn't anyone of your family, either."

"No." His face was shuttered, gazing past me to

the window, and I wondered with a faint sense of shock whether his family even knew he'd remarried. I was nerving myself to ask, because I'd already learned in the office that NO expression—meaning a subject was closed—but surely a wife was different? I opened my mouth—and a stewardess was smiling cordially beside us.

"Dom Sebastiao, so good to see you again. You permit me to offer the good wishes of the crew for your happiness?" She'd brought Seb's usual scotch, another for me. "So many Norte-Americanos prefer, I took a chance," she said shyly, "but if not right, I can quickly change."

"Exactly right, thank you." I smiled at her, but the moment to ask about Seb's family was lost.

Perhaps it was as well. A honeymoon should be unclouded, but it shouldn't be a bore. Seb was the refutation of Latins are lousy lovers (not that I'd any basis for comparison, but if you're content with anything, why look for trouble?)—but he was busy all day. I knew no one in Rio; we were staying in a fully staffed villa that ran itself, and June in Portugal is winter in Brazil, too chilly for beach clubs, often too rainy even for walking, which is the best way to learn a city.

When Seb was exasperated by an inaccurate translation, I said, "Bring 'em home; it'll give me something to do."

"My wife does not work!" He had that NO look, but this time I was perverse.

"Oh, piffle," I said contemptuously. "Who's to know? You're cutting off your nose to spite your face! Last week I was batting out this stuff for you every day; if I was competent then, I'm competent now. Get me a typewriter and paper, tell 'em you've found a better translator—because frankly, if I have to look at that damned hill, or knit another sweater I'll never wear, I'll go stir crazy!"

Seb looked at me curiously. "You would really not object to typing for hours—on your honeymoon?"

"A wife helps her husband wherever and however she can," I said slowly. "Doesn't she, Seb? I expect I won't have time when I begin being Dona dos Martim, but right now I'm available—and correct me if I'm wrong," I added courteously, "but this is your honeymoon, too, is it not? And you are spending hours in an office every day . . ."

He considered it for the space of a highball. "Very well, *querida*. Apparently I have something to learn about marriage, too."

Now there was a new fascination about the work: it concerned me, even if indirectly—although less so than I'd thought. Seb came in one evening as I finished a final page, and handed me a legal envelope. "Your marriage settlements, *queridinho*," he said casually. "Send them to your father for safekeeping." He stretched wearily. "Come, it's time for a drink."

"One page more . . ."

He leaned against the doorjamb, lighting a cigarette while I typed briskly, ripped the paper from the machine and tossed it into a file box. "I'll collate tomorrow. Did you mention a drink?"

"You enjoy this, don't you?"

"It's what I know best," I shrugged, sliding the cover over the machine. "After all, I knew your business before I knew you!"

"Yes. What will you do without it when we get home?"

"I'll be busier than ever," I said in surprise. "There's the house to decorate, Duarte to ready for school, I thought I might go on overnight trips with you—to be company, unless you like to be alone." I got up, went over to lean within the curve of his arm.

"I detest being alone!"

"There's all your friends to meet, and planning how to conquer Lisbon society so your position will be upheld," I frowned absently. "I think I'll do best with dinners, unless your wife ought not to know how to cook. Otherwise, I thought I might build a reputation for special dishes. D'you think that would be all right?"

"I think you will set Lisbon on its ears," he said. "What else?"

"Would you terribly much mind," I asked in a very small voice, "if I had a baby?"

His arm tightened so convulsively I nearly cried out. Then he relaxed, laying his cheek on my hair. "The very thing," he said admiringly. "Why didn't I think of it before!" His hand gently stroked my cheek. "I should like a child from you more than anything in the world, but not yet, Persis. Wait a year, give yourself time to establish."

"I could wait two years if necessary, but I do want babies."

"It will not be so long, only trust me a while," he murmured.

Unconsciously I twisted, raising my head, hoping to be kissed—but Seb was staring over my head into space, his fingers still caressing my cheek, but his face . . .

He is a devil, and the family is accursed.

chapter 4

We would stay in the apartment while I redecorated Seb's house. We would spend a week at Casa Carranca in August. We would go to the States, taking Duarte to be outfitted and started in boarding school. By dint of superhuman wire-pulling, daddy had achieved acceptance of Seb's son at Phillips Andover, contingent upon his showing in the massive sheaf of tests they'd sent us.

I looked over the questions with awe. Had I ever been able to answer them? Presumably I had, since I'd made Phi Bete junior year at Radcliffe, but I'd not only had the advantage of a scholarly father; I was American and understood the language. Could a ten-year-old Portuguese boy cope with such hard questions in a strange language? Seb had no doubts. "Of course Duarte will be satisfactory. He's had excellent tutors. If he's acceptable to Eton," Seb stated arrogantly, "he'll easily manage this Andover."

"Hmmm, don't be so sure," I advised, tossing a

couple of tests into his lap. "Can you answer any of those?"

He studied the papers, frowning slightly. "What is an Appomattox?"

"Exactly!" I said, triumphantly. "If you don't know, when you've the advantage of having been in America, how d'you think Duarte will? Daddy wrote you there's a dozen applicants for every place in every school. The best he could do was get Duarte a chance, and he's starting with a handicap, because American kids are taught in a different order. They don't get Latin or Greek until high school. Right now, they have more science and math, but Duarte has to know what American children have been learning, or he'll never be able to keep up.

"He's acceptable to Eton because all the others have had the same training method, but I warn you, darling, our schools are very different. Duarte may easily have to go to Eton, after all—and if so, it'll be for his good."

"What are you talking about?" Seb asked, startled. "I want my son to attend an American school. I've the money, he's been well-grounded . . . if they find he needs special tutoring for any subject, I'll pay for it, until he pulls level with the others."

"Yes, well, they won't agree."

Seb regarded me intently. "Explain this, if you please."

I collected my thoughts for a moment. "I said our schools were different," I began, slowly, "but it's because we think differently about children. Your money doesn't matter, Seb. No American school will take Duarte if he's going to have problems with his homework, because they consider the child first, and they're right! Duarte may be intelligent, well-bred and well-grounded—but what he *is* is a small boy, who'll be thousands of miles from home, coping with strangers in an unfamiliar language, trying to make friends and maybe being rebuffed or humiliated if he makes a funny mistake in his English. Little boys sometimes are little beasts. Were you happy at Eton, Seb?"

I had the answer in the sudden tightening of his lips. "Not at first, but I settled down very rapidly." I wondered fleetingly what scars that adjustment had left. Whose fag had Sebastiao been, what sort of treatment had he had from that older boy?

"Any American school will think first about adjustment, possible homesickness," I said quietly. "That's why daddy insisted on Andover, so Duarte will have friendly people close at hand . . . and it's one reason the school agreed. I have nieces and nephews about his age, who'll be kind and help him get used to Americans. That's enough load for a small child. If he can't do the work easily enough to give him self-confidence, it will all be too much for him. He'll get discouraged at the outset, and no matter how he reacts—whether he gives up, or forces himself to superhuman efforts—it will be bad for him."

It didn't get across. Seb reared back stiffly. "My son is unlikely to 'give up,' as you put it. I appreciate your family's willingness to invite him for a weekend, but I see no reason for pampering the boy."

"It isn't pampering, Seb," I tried again. "I expect daddy will explain it better than I can . . . but you don't want Duarte to develop some sort of neurosis or complex, for heaven's sake."

"Absurd! The boy is of an age to be sent away to school, so I shall send him, that's all. It is the responsibility of the school to educate him correctly. If extra help is needed, I will provide it."

I looked at his stubborn face in despair. "All right, darling—but couldn't he come here for a couple of days, so I could tell if he needs a bit of emphasis somewhere before he takes the tests? We could put a cot in the study."

Seb stood up, tossing the papers on the table. "No," he said with finality. "Not now, and don't suggest it again, if you please. You will meet Duarte in good time. I'm appreciative of your desire to mother my son, but at the moment—after only a few weeks of marriage," he shrugged, "no doubt it's selfish of me, but I still wish to enjoy your undivided attention. You have enough to do, to get us out of this cramped apartment by fall, without an active child underfoot." He stalked away toward the study, while I swallowed hard to prevent tears.

"I didn't mean, I only thought I could help him, Seb," I whispered. "You want him to go to school in America —two days isn't long." I don't think he even heard me. He was already closing the study door, leaving me bewildered. I stared blindly at the flowering trees flung over the hill before me, feeling as though I'd somehow hurt Seb . . . I sensed a note of pain, despite the arrogance of his words.

Why should he speak so cuttingly of a perfectly natural wish to meet his son? Did he not care for the boy for some reason? Yes, we were still newlyweds and there was only one bathroom—but Duarte could have a *pot de chambre* for night use, and Seb was gone from ten to six, leaving plenty of time for baths and general hygiene. Dully, I accepted ineptitude on my part. Somehow, I'd supposed once returned from the formal wedding trip, life would begin to be normal. We'd be a family unit, getting acquainted, and my stepson would visit us to be assured he'd be part of it . . . but this was Portugal and my husband was fifteen years older than I.

I asked nothing better than to concentrate on Seb, to be sure every smallest detail—whether dinner menu or unstarched shirt collars—was exactly to his liking . . . and the very first thing, I'd been stupid. I'd forgotten foreign children are nursery-trained, do not become part of their families until old enough for instruction in adult manners. Instinctively, in trying to explain a possible rejection by Andover, I'd applied American standards that Seb would neither understand nor accept. No wonder he was irritated—although why should he be hurt?

I'd said I didn't know how to be married, and I'd flunked the first test, but there would be no more mistakes. I lit a cigarette, determinedly. I would question nothing until I'd learned the expectable reactions of a rich, older, foreign aristocrat. It was more important for me to learn the requirements for being a correct wife in Portugal than to be mom-ish about a boy I didn't even know, who was probably a bullet-headed little roughneck who'd lick every kid in the school if they so much as stared at him cross-eyed!

"Persis?" Seb called from the doorway. "I have said we will join Paul and Maria at Figaro tonight, there is a new dancer. You can be ready at eight?"

"Yes." I smiled at him. "Oh, are you off?"

"To the office for a half hour." He raised his hand in a wave, and vanished, to return a moment later, leaning from the door, his expression one of eager interest. "Persis, *queridinho*—what is an Appomatox, anyway?"

"What do you think it is? And I warn you it is not related to a machete or a mattock."

His face broke into a wicked grin. "Shall I confess? I have looked it up! It is a courthouse somewhere in your state of Virginia," he strode forward and bent to kiss me, "and I have not the least idea whether or not my son will be aware of this! We can only hope for the best, but when I forward the tests to Mr. Wilson, I shall suggest intensive review of American history. Will it content you, *querida?*"

"Of course. I was only meaning to be helpful." I pulled him toward me for another kiss, feeling vaguely elated. In a way, it was a tacit apology. I felt warm all over, as he went away, and even more determined to control my American reactions. Least said, soonest mended—not that I could ever be a doormat, but this incident proved to me that Seb was receptive, trying to understand me as I wanted to understand him. I smiled to myself over his ingenious way of smoothing the tiny difference between us. "What *is* an Appomattox?" I chuckled; daddy would appreciate that! He'd probably ask Seb for permission to appropriate it, to use in some erudite article. I could hardly wait for my family to inspect Seb in person. I knew they'd accept anyone who made me happy, just as they'd accepted one of my sister's husbands who was an absolute *nudnick,* sweet-tempered as he was. So long as Sue was content, we'd endure—even welcome wholeheartedly—a man whose entire ambition was to be a master sergeant for Uncle Sam's quartermaster division!

But when I presented Sebastiao . . . The whole family was going to adore him at once, I knew it. Daddy would get him alone in the study for academic discussions; my brothers would be impressed by his business ability; Lucy would enjoy his quick wit, and he'd instantly be welcomed on his own merits, quite apart from making me happy. Nor had I any doubts that Seb would equally enjoy my family. It was a major happiness to anticipate next month, and meanwhile, let Seb order our lives.

I'd never yearned to be anything but a weak little woman who could be tucked in a breast pocket. He rarely decreed anything with which I didn't agree, and after my resistance in Brazil (which got us two spare days of sun in Teneriffe), he was willing to listen to a mild objection, alternative suggestion. He still mostly said NO, but who cared how he phrased things? Once on the agenda, I was on my own to carry out. He wished no consultation, no communiqués. Upon insistent probing, he looked over his newspaper with faint impatience. *"Por deus,* I do NOT like yellow, nor spindly furniture! Does that satisfy you?"

"Partly. How much money shall I spend?"

"Whatever it costs, *querida."* He went back to the paper, and I felt faintly impatient, myself.

"Suppose it turns out to be a hundred thousand dollars?" He looked up at that! "It is to be a palace?" He raised his eyebrows in awe, while I giggled. Smiling, he drew me down beside him. "You are the businesswoman, who likes a budget?"

"Yes, please."

"Then: whatever it costs to please you, that is your budget."

But if he wouldn't look at samples or tell me preferences? "Suppose you don't like it when I get through?" I asked uneasily.

Seb looked at me for a long moment. "You must stop this self-doubt, *minha mulher,"* he remarked. "I shall like whatever you like—and if I do not," he shrugged, "we will have it done over. I am rich enough to indulge my whims."

That he was.

The envelope I'd sent daddy from Brazil contained a half-million bucks of blue chip securities, plus life interests in the Lisbon house and Casa Carranca. There were provisions for possible children, and five thousand acres of Amazon jungle. "What will I do with *that?*"

"Build a retirement home and fish for piranhas?" But while I laughed, he said seriously, "Hang onto it, Persis, it's good acreage for early development along the river."

Now it's over and resolved, I sometimes recall those first weeks with a kind of disbelief. We were so happy, so carelessly gay, with never enough hours for all I wanted to do, so that each day was expectancy, achievement, anticipation of tomorrow, all wrapped in laughter and kisses. Yet all the while, each of us was so close to the truth. If we'd pooled our knowledge, would it have made any difference? All that still seems incredible is the speed: as though the powder train were already laid, the jigsaw puzzle complete but for a single piece.

How could anyone know I was it, least of all me? I was in love with being a woman, a wife. Most of all, I was in love with my husband.

When did I realize my love was not returned? Even more, how did I know this? There was no one moment or look, yet very slowly I knew Seb's approval of anything I suggested was not doting fondness but indifference. He did not care what I did, providing it did not inconvenience him.

Flying home from Teneriffe, I said, "Dorica Andreas was my first friend in Lisbon. May I invite her to the apartment, or shall I meet her elsewhere?"

"Invite her by all means—but perhaps, when I am not home; she might find it embarrassing."

Hesitantly, I asked, "Hadn't I better know the problem, now?"

"She's the illegitimate daughter of my brother-in-law's younger sister, Elvira Revascues," he said calmly, "which makes her my third cousin. She contends there was a marriage, but no proof exists. Spanish Civil War," he shrugged, "when the smoke cleared, everyone was dead—and suddenly there's a baby girl! Very embarrassing for Miguel, who'd just married my sister," Seb chuckled. "No question she's Elvira's child, she's the image of her mother. She's got the family ring, she was living with her grandmother until Cousin Annunciata died. Miguel couldn't get around that, but he won't acknowledge legitimacy."

"Why not?" I could tell Seb enjoyed Miguel's predicament.

"If she were legitimate, she'd automatically inherit Elvira's half of the Revascues properties, and by Miguel's standard, there wasn't enough to go round as it was." He snorted contemptuously. "All they asked was education money; the lawyers advised Miguel it wouldn't commit him to pay it—and by then, he'd got Branca's dowry in his hands, but he wouldn't part with a penny."

Seb's lips slowly curved into a sardonic smile. "By all means, continue the friendship, *querida*. Dorica Andreas is your third cousin by marriage, with or without benefit of clergy." He laughed heartily. "Tell her I completely approve."

Much later it occurred to me that Seb's approval was meant for the discomfiture of his brother-in-law.

I'd written Laura she could keep the apartment, including beds, but I was sending packers for everything else. There was a voluminous letter on Saturday morning: "She says if she has beds, the place is furnished, movers have been and gone, she's sent a box of small treasures at once—how kind of her," I flipped the page and said, "Good heavens!"

"She has established a connection with the superintendent, or one of the beds is already broken," Seb murmured, tickling Shadrach lazily.

"Really, Seb! Laura's perfectly respectable; she just doesn't get married because divorces cost so much."

"This suspense is unbearable," he complained.

"Poochy and Artie have split!" I announced impressively. "At Trentini's. Somehow he dropped a beer mug and her eye was in the way, she got a shiner, couldn't be photographed for Miss Rheingold next day, and has left him forever." I refolded the letter and laughed heartily.

"So he is free again. What became of the zircon?"

Another world, another life . . . "What *did* I do with it?"

"It was not returned?"

"A birthday present, not an engagement ring—that was the whole point. Shadrach," I remembered. "I hung it on his collar."

"Why?" Seb's fingers moved through the cat's ruff, gently unfastened the collar, slid the ring into his hand, refastened while Shadrach stretched lazily.

I looked vaguely at the ring, turned for scrutiny. "Because he didn't like it on his tail. It seemed a good idea at the time."

"It does match your eyes; a sapphire would be better."
With a flick of the long slender fingers, Seb threw it over
his shoulder into the hillside shrubbery. "Shall we go to
Cascaes for dinner, *querida?* Or would you like to swim
and I will call for you? There are papers in the study or
I would go with you."

I stared silently at the clump into which the ring had
fallen, until Seb looked up. "You cannot decide?"

"Cascaes—I've things to do, also . . ." I wanted to say,
"Hey, that was my life you threw away," but that was
absurd. My life was here, with the man I loved.

All the same, I thought he might have asked me first.

Random thoughts while I washed my hair or lay sun-
ning on the terrace became a Conga line of idle *non
sequiturs,* turning into two and two equals four—
plus X.

We'd both talked to my parents before the wedding;
no one had represented Seb's family in person. Under-
standable an elderly arthritic mother and half-blind sister
wouldn't drive 150 miles—but surely there was a telephone at Carranca? There was a huge pile of letters and
wires, wishing us happiness—even a few wedding pres-
ents, waiting when we got home. They included no message from Carranca.

Was Dona Benedecta unwilling to recognize an Epis-
copalian foreigner? Had Sebastiao even officially informed his mother? If not, a civil ceremony would make
it possible for her to ignore my existence. He'd said we
would visit Carranca next month, to take Duarte to
America—but when I arrived would Dona Benedecta
be "visiting" elsewhere? That would be no more wound-
ing than this disdainful silence. Had Seb expected this
reaction?

I couldn't ask. From the beginning he spoke warmly of my family, looked forward to meeting them, loudly demanded every bit of news in home letters—but at mention of Casa Carranca, he shuttered his face and changed the subject—and so did Teresa.

She waited on Seb hand and foot, silently anticipating his every wish—yet once I glimpsed her face, glancing back as she opened the kitchen door. Her expression was almost frightened.

With me, she was occasionally chatty. She made touching efforts to please, but there was a look in her eye as she said, *"sim, sim,* Dona Persis," as though she were sorry for me . . .

The lower apartment was regularly aired and dusted by Teresa. Perhaps Dona Benedecta planned a formal presentation of me, on her next visit to Lisbon? Several times I'd been aware of soft lights and movement downstairs, although Teresa said no one had used the place in seven years, and *faça favor,* would I inspect the draperies that were beginning to rot?

Startled, I protested, "Someone's been there, I've heard them." Teresa shook her head stubbornly. "No one, Dona. I would know. It must be from the next house you hear sounds."

I was equally convinced the lower apartment *had* been used, although not since we'd returned from Brazil. Were there other Martim or Antobal relatives who might use the apartment for a night in preference to a hotel? Perhaps Teresa's "no one" only referred to Dona Benedecta herself . . .

The house in which we would live told its own story: a correct town residence with innumerable rooms, all very neat and well-aired—but aside from a study, bedroom and bath on the second floor, it was passive as Snow White. Following the elderly manservant from room to room, making measurements for scale drawings, I was increasingly puzzled. Had anyone ever lived here? There were a few spots on the dining room carpet, a cigarette burn on a salon table; otherwise the house slept, needing only a touch to awaken it.

Admittedly, the decor was florid, but there were good pieces. Seb had decreed I was to redecorate entirely, retain nothing; my thrifty New England soul whispered temptingly, "Put the Boule cabinet upstairs—would he ever know?"

On the top floor, bunnies and teddy bears scampered about the wallpaper, but the nursery furniture was gone. I took a second glance, and realized there'd never been any! No child had ever played here; the place was as the paperhanger had left it. Then, where did Duarte sleep when he visited his father?

I found guestrooms and baths; one showed signs of use, furnished with an antique shaving stand. I saw no trace anywhere of a small boy.

The suite matching Seb's was close-shuttered. "The sun is strongest here, we keep the blinds drawn," Joao swiftly threw back draperies, opened casements, while I looked about me and identified X . . .

Both morning and bedroom were hung in yellow silk, furnished in authentic Louis Quatorze. The dressing room was pale yellow panelling and gold-framed antique mirrors; the bath, a confection of lemon ice with gilded fittings. All was a dainty bonbon to surround a tiny brunette bride.

I snapped shut the folding rule, stuffed it into my briefcase. "Thank you, Joao. I'll—come back tomorrow." Blindly, I turned and stumbled down the main stairs.

I'd said a previous marriage didn't matter. Seb never mentioned Cristinha. Until today she had been a shadow; now she was alive. I pictured Seb, sitting in those silent rooms, remembering parties, dinners, shared nights in the delicately painted bed under a yellow silk coverlet.

I drew the car to the curb, leaned my head on the steering wheel, fighting tears. Why, after nine years, should he have married me? Because he wanted a woman he did not love?

The Curse!

I'd forgotten he was "forever doomed to lose what he loved best in life." He'd loved Cristinha and lost her; now he was taking no chances. In a way, it even explained his impersonal decisions for Duarte.

Shakily I lit a cigarette and tried to think positive. What if he didn't love me as wildly as I loved him? I had everything else a woman could want, not only material things but respect, kindness, affection. He used terms of endearment, he made love to me frequently, almost hungrily. He said my eyes were bluer than the sky, my hair was corn silk, my skin was white velvet.

He'd never said, quite simply, "I love you."

Yet why should I have assumed it? What could there be about Persis Bradbury to evoke love from a brilliant handsome rich man already experienced in love, who could certainly have his choice of women anywhere, any time? How naive can you be! I'd been incredulous at my luck, that I could see him over morning coffee cups, feel him next to me each night.

I was right to be incredulous.

With a long breath, I got out of the car, went into the tiled apartment entrance hall. Dimly I heard movement behind the lower door: Teresa dusting and airing. I was in no mood to inspect draperies. I went up the stairs, tossed purse and gloves onto the hall table and went out to the terrace—to stop short. "Renée!"

"Oui, c'est moi." She uncurled herself lazily, got up to kiss me affectionately. "We arrive in the middle of the night as usual. Luis is at the office, so I come to see for myself." She sank back on the lounge, eyeing my black opal set with alternate canary and white diamonds. *"Enfin,* it is true you have married him. When Luis told me, I could not believe . . ."

"He'd fall for a homely American secretary fifteen years his junior?" Well, I couldn't believe it either, not any longer.

"Oh, you're not unattractive, *chérie;* the bone structure is excellent," she assured me, literally. "You will last far better than I, because you have not arrived as yet."

I laughed helplessly, while she hauled out the inevitable Balkan Sobranies. "You think he should have waited until I arrived?"

She took her time lighting the cigarette. "No," she said, finally, "I think you should, Persis." She sighed, while I was fumbling for my own cigarettes. *"Alors,* I suppose it was irresistible to exchange a zircon for an opal and a title in only a month. I told Luis we should not allow this running away, but he said Sebastiao was in France—and even when it was known he'd returned, how could one dream . . ." She shook her head sadly. *"Enfin,* what is done is done, and perhaps it will answer.

I help you all I can while I am here—and how did you like Brazil?"

I wasn't ready to remember Brazil, or the honeymoon I now knew was only for one. Was this how it appeared to the world? Persis Bradbury was jilted in New York, you know, so she went abroad and married a Portuguese widower old enough to be her father. Wonder how she got him? It was the ultimate humiliation. "Is that what you think?"

"Not at all," Renée said, slowly. "If anything, I think Sebastiao has the best of it. He has caught a charming, well-bred young woman on the rebound, and married her before she knows enough about him to say 'No, thank you very much.'"

"What should I have known? That he still loves Cristinha?"

She stared at me in absolute amazement. "Did you think he was carrying the torch? Oh, *merde alors,* you are a simpleton, Persis!" She laughed heartily, "For nine years he has the cake and eats it too! A son—for the name—he's rid of the invalid wife, free as a bird, highly eligible . . . *mon Dieu,* the women who tried for him! If Caterina dos Passos had not been killed skiing, she might have got him; otherwise, he is a Houdini, *je t'assure!*

"*Vois-tu, mignonne,* enough is as good as a feast—not that one wished Cristinha to die so tragically," Renée rattled on, "but if anything kept him single it was his taste of marriage! One respects him for honoring his father's contract when the family was grown poor, permissible to repudiate. Oh, was Dona Benedecta in a tantrum that he should 'waste himself' only for land in Brazil!"

"You mean it was *mariage de convenance?* They

didn't—love each other?" I had to get that straight.

"Not in your sentimental American sense," Renée
shook her head. "Oh, she thought herself *supremely* fortunate to get him for so small a *dot,* and he was a good
husband. He endured the aches and pains, the whining
stupidity; he was always courteous and considerate."
She glanced at me shrewdly. *"Ne t'en fache pas, chérie,"*
she advised, bluntly. "You are entirely different."

"Yes. I expect you wonder how I pulled it off."

Renée revolved the cigarette lighter in her fingers absently. "I do not think you did, and so I shall say to anyone who asks," she said, finally. "It was simply something that *happened* to you: a charming man of the
world exactly when you were most susceptible, although," her eyes narrowed reflectively, *"je me de-
mande . . ."*

"Why me," I finished. "Yes, I wonder, too."

She pursed her lips. "He could get you no other way?"

"He never tried. He'd have had no trouble . . ."

"Comme ça?" Her eyebrows twitched, while Teresa
emerged with the bar tray. So she was finished downstairs, the time must be five, with Seb due shortly—how
was I to greet him? I fixed drinks and said baldly, "Help
me?"

Renée sampled her drink, made a face and hastily
added another spoonful of sugar, eyeing me critically
while she stirred. "You are the type he's always liked,"
she mused. "Blue eyes, blonde hair—perhaps he wishes
to settle. It is easier to come home every night than to
be crawling in and out of windows at his age, after all."

I wasn't offended by her Gallic earthiness. "So far he
likes coming home every night."

She shrugged. "He chooses a healthy young woman to
decorate bed and home, who adores him, will make

every effort to please, who will be a magnificent step-mamma for Duarte and may give him other children . . ."
Renée grinned at me mockingly. *"P'tite gosse!* Does it occur to you that perhaps he married you because he likes having you around?" She laughed heartily. *"Enfin,* who knows why a man marries, least of all the man himself. *Sans doute,* Sebastiao has his reasons, and if he is like most men—which one must admit he is not," she observed thoughtfully, "he cannot explain in words. *Ne t'en fache pas,"* she repeated, "play it by ear, Persis, and you'll do very well, but," she sat up abruptly, *"stay away from Casa Carranca!"*

"Why?" I asked, feeling a throb of fear at her expression.

"It's—evil. Those mountains, never more than a few rays of sun." She shivered. "Things happen, to make you almost believe that curse. Cristinha, going to the nursery in the middle of the night and tripping over the cord of her bathrobe . . . Branca, with a reputation for medieval art restoration, and all is ended by a detached retina because her husband, that pig Miguel Revascues, cannot hold his wine and smashes the car into a stone wall . . . Caterina, killed skiing when a snow slide hurls a pebble to her temple—and in the middle of it all, the old Spanish tarantula, with all the threads in her claws, spinning them out and reeling them in," Renée spat venomously.

Dimly I could hear voices as I sat transfixed by Renée's compelling gaze—Seb and Luis entering the hall. She leaned forward urgently, "Stay away from Carranca, Persis," she whispered. "Stay away, if you value your life!"

chapter 5

Gradually I achieved a minor Nepenthe, in which I accepted everything at face value. Renée was not to be drawn farther, was faintly impatient, "Who cares why the old beast ignores you? The longer, the better, *je t'assure!* What shall you wear to the Limons'?"

Superficially nothing was changed, life was only enhanced by Luis and Renée. Nightly, we dined on the terrace, sat over coffee and liqueurs in soft-scented darkness, while the men reminisced wickedly until we were weak from laughter. So few days past I'd have shared Seb's pleasure in his friend wholeheartedly; now it was only an invisible umbrella beneath which I cowered to draw breath. I dreaded the future, when Luis and Renée would be gone. Somehow I must be adjusted to reality, by then.

Meanwhile, Renée was a powerhouse, introducing me to Lisbon society and hailing the redecoration with glee. I had ample confirmation of her thumbnail sketch: I was the greatest possible contrast to Cristinha, and welcomed with open arms. I took pains to be liked; Dona dos

Martim would be happy to serve on committees, join a bridge club, play golf, or sponsor a charity ball.

Slowly, I evolved a tentative program: I would not embarrass Seb by undue display of my love, I would make do with whatever affection he offered, and I would concentrate on being a wife to gain and hold his respect and admiration.

Already the mystery of the static house was solved: there had never been any gay parties! "Once a year, a formal invitation—one says 'yes,' and makes other arrangements, knowing all will be cancelled at the last moment because Cristinha is moping . . ." So I would turn the dos Martim house into the most desired invitation in Lisbon, constantly filled with guests who'd be served the most delicious food—even if I had to cook it myself.

Almost feverishly, I commanded the place be stripped: every drapery, picture, rug, chair, was to go. "Go where?" Renée asked, startled. "You are not serious? The servants will only sell and pocket the money, Persis!"

"Let them. You don't suggest Dona dos Martim should sell and pocket, do you?"

"You are right, of course—but in that case," she said briskly, "I have long admired that Boule cabinet, and the servants will not know its value . . ."

"Have it crated tomorrow, sweetie. Anything else you fancy?" I suppressed a grin at her literal interpretation, while I dealt with the contractor. "All ceilings white, strip all wall papers, remove all bathroom tiles, rewire for air-conditioning and a modern kitchen, refinish all wood floors . . ." She came back at last with a long list and eyed me curiously.

"I hope you know what you're doing, *chérie;* such sweeping changes will cost a fortune."

I nodded indifferently. "I have no budget."

"Tiens, one knew he was rich, *mais tout de même . . ."*

"I suggested it might cost a hundred thousand; he didn't wince."

Renée's eyes sparkled. "I help you! Please, Persis? *Hein,* no budget! Hah! Let us go to Paris for wall paper, I know a little man," she wheedled, "and there is nothing to do here, after all, with these stupid mergers. They'll never know we've gone."

I was brushing my hair when Seb padded in from the shower and bent to kiss my neck. To control the instant response of my heart, I said at random, "D'you mind if I go to Paris tomorrow? René knows a wall paper designer."

He straightened up, and in the mirror his expression was oddly controlled. Catching my eye, he smiled faintly. "So—the palace begins to emerge and there is nothing fine enough in Lisbon? By all means go to Paris, *querida.* Enjoy yourself."

"You will really not mind? You are so occupied at the moment, and you have Luis for company . . ."

"Oh, I shall not be lonely," he laughed, "and I must be very occupied indeed, if whatever I make with one hand you will spend from the other."

We went to Paris, and to Stockholm, Copenhagen, London for a look-see that produced a hunt table for the dining room window curve. The price was shocking; Renée raised one eyebrow. "You have no budget, buy it!" I did. If all I'd have was a house, it might as well be a palace.

I might as well be a princess while I was about it. I

bought some clothes in Paris, taking what pride I could in Renée's respect for my selection. Flying home to Lisbon for the Limons' party, I stared blindly from the window while she catnapped. For ten days I'd put Seb out of my mind, concentrated on inspecting, choosing, coordinating. Not hard. I was equally out of his mind. No matter where we were, Luis telephoned Renée each night; all I got were messages, "Seb says to enjoy yourself."

I had not enjoyed myself. I'd spent a terrifying amount of money as wisely as I knew how—but if he didn't like the results, he'd have it done over. Face it: Seb didn't care where I was nor what doing. Had he even found the unshared bed inconvenient? No, I decided drearily or he'd have summoned me home—and God help me, I'd have taken the next plane. I was wild to get back to him, but if I weren't even sexually necessary, we were back to the basic question. Why had he married me?

Five o'clock, an empty apartment, although Teresa and Shadrach welcomed me cordially. Infinitesimal signs: a damp towel, a crumpled tie on the floor. *"Sim, sim,* Dom Sebastiao has dressed, but there is a conference, he returns for you at seven."

Letters from home, and Laura's box of "special treasures"—I had no heart to open it. It was an effort even to read the mail, the loving messages for my husband. Lying in the warm bath, I thought frantically, "We can't go next month, mother will guess . . ."

I put on one of the Paris gowns, sapphire blue silk designed à la grecque, to cling when I stood, flow when I moved. Dimly I heard voices: Teresa showing Renée and Luis to the terrace—and cutting across the babble, the deep commanding resonance that was Sebastiao. I gripped the edge of the dressing table, waiting . . . and all voices, all movement receded into silence. After a moment, I set a drop of perfume here and there, stood up and inspected myself in the long mirror. There was no hurry after all, if my husband could wait to greet me among guests after a ten-day absence.

The color of the silk intensified my eyes to amazing depths. The zircon no longer matched the eyes of Dona Persis dos Martim. Twitching a fold of the silk smoothly, I thought drily that the cost of this dress was probably more than a real sapphire. I opened the bedroom door and went calmly forward, seeing the length of the hall to a sort of animated "still life." Renée, splash of hibiscus red sparked with diamonds, Luis's portly figure stuffed into dinner clothes, leaning gallantly to light her cigarette, Teresa, offering canapés—and towering above and behind, a tall figure lounging against the wall, laughing, at ease, utterly content to wait until his possession chose to appear.

I stood in the doorway, beneath terrace lights, and said, "Good evening—may I have a drink, too, Teresa?"

Vaguely, I heard Renée: *"Magnifique!* The color, the fit, superb, *mignonne!"* and Luis, "My dear Persis, you are a goddess! Seb, how are you so fortunate as to marry Venus herself?"

I was aware only of my husband, motionless for a moment, then lazily unfolding himself and coming toward me with a smile. He held out his arms, and I went into them with no hesitation. How abject can a woman be? But with Seb's arms around me, his lips on mine, I didn't care if I had to grovel on the floor when he tired of me.

That moment was not yet; I could still make his breath quick and hot, make him tighten his arms, until he murmured, *"Por deus,* you go to my head, *minha coraçao*. After ten days—ah, you will pay for this later, *queridinho!*"

"Only fair to warn you I'm broke to the wide, nothing left but the lily-white body," I murmured in return. Seb's dark eyes kindled, but before he could say anything, Luis was calling, "Here, you two, time enough for that later. Return from Olympus, if you please!"

Seb swung around, his arm holding me close. "This is no goddess," he laughed exultantly, "This is *minha bruxa com olho d'azul!*"

Luis smiled at me. "I'll drink to that," he said, raising his glass. "Renée?"

In the tiny silence while they drank, there was a tinkling crash, and Teresa was staring at me, ashen-faced, my highball glass in splinters at her feet. *"Desulpe,* my hand slips," she whispered, scuttling away to the kitchen, as Luis wandered forward to replenish his drink, chatting casually with Seb.

I stood bewildered, yet feeling an eerie tingling. Why should Teresa—who was incredibly efficient, neat-fingered, who never damaged anything—why should Teresa break a glass, because Seb called me his blue-eyed witch? Unconsciously, I looked after her, and in the kitchen doorway her eyes met mine briefly.

In the gathering dimness, they held the dumb awed reverence I'd sometimes seen in peasants kneeling before a wayside shrine.

Renée visited her sister in Majorca; Luis and Seb went to Oporto. "You will not object, *querida?* After all, I was alone for ten days." The dark eyes were teasing.

"Of course not, I shall be up to my ears in chandeliers."

"In fact, you will not know I am gone, nor miss me at all?"

"On the contrary, I shall miss you every moment of each day—and each second of every night."

"*Fetiçeria,* you almost convince me . . ."

I opened my mouth to say, *"Why* do you keep calling me a witch? What's the meaning?" but he'd withdrawn his arms, rolled aside to reach for a cigarette, "Did the white dinner jacket return from the cleaners?"

"Yes"—but the moment was gone.

Now it was I, alone in Lisbon, inspecting progress at the house each day, but only a mess of rewiring, new pipes, overlaid by a strong odor of paint. Impossible to know whether it would ever approximate my mind's eye when I'd chosen the colors and fabrics—one wondered if it would ever even reach that point.

Now I opened Laura's box of "small treasures," and sat laughing over the absurd items she'd included: three vegetable steamer baskets, a parsley mincer, a battered thesaurus, an Orrefors vase I'd got for a quarter its original price due to a disastrous chipped corner . . . and finally, swathed in cotton batting, Uncle Ted's triptych and the miniature of Old Persis Herself.

In the brilliant Iberian sunshine, her blue eyes stared at me expressionlessly, beneath the rigid goffered frill of cap hiding every vestige of hair. It was probably white; faded ink on the back said 1747, when she was nearly seventy. The artist had done his best, but it was not possible entirely to conceal the scrawny neck, the bleached cheek bones. Only the eyes were still young, vividly blue as rain-drenched Ragged Robins . . . what would she think if she knew her descendant was being called a witch?

I chuckled to myself, thinking I'd get a new frame:

very plain wood, but pointed in gold, and old Persis should have an honored spot in my new home. Propping the miniature against my iced tea glass, I gently opened the triptych, feasting my eyes on the faded colors. I knew only that it was very old and authentic, that Uncle Ted loved it like a talisman. It went everywhere with him, he'd been used to open the doors and set it beside him at night—as though it kept him company.

The one time I'd asked about it was the summer I was eleven and acquired a nightmare due to unlimited barbecue. I paddled out to the ranch living room in search of adult reassurance. Uncle Ted cuddled me, wiped away tears. "What's that?" I asked.

He drew on his pipe till it glowed. "All that's left of my life," he said, reaching a long arm to the highball glass.

"I don't understand. You're alive now, aren't you?"

"Yes, but everyone has many lives, and some are gained but more are lost."

"Is it something in the Bible?"

"In a way. See," he pulled me upright on his lap, leaned to turn the triptych to the lamplight, "there is Mary with the Babe, here are the Wise Men with their gifts, and on this side is Joseph. Those are angels behind him."

"It's hard to see, isn't it?"

"That's because it's so very old. Just think: someone painted that hundreds of years ago, far across the sea, and now we are still enjoying it."

"Where did it come from?"

"Spain. My dearest friend gave it to me to keep for her, there are only two in the world."

"What happened to your friend?"

"She—died. And if you do not stop your 'satiable curiosity, and go to bed, young Persis, I shall be dead before morning. Scoot!"

I'd had the triptych in my apartment for five years, I'd never looked at it closely until now. Closed, the carved wooden panels that were dark and smooth with age were meant to represent the great doors of some medieval cathedral—the tiny carved projections were spires.

Within was muted peace, but for the first time I saw flowers, smiling cherubs, birds and beasts—everything indispensable to the harmony of the whole, yet worthy of individual notice. Even the animals of the Wise Men were personalities: one, dull-eyed, thinking only of his supper, one pawing the ground, meditating a bolt to unseat the fattish man on his back, and bringing up the rear, a docile she-ass, whose rider was so confident as to hold the reins in one hand while the other hung casually at his side.

On that hand was a diamond-shaped gold seal ring . . .

Even under a magnifying glass I wasn't sure it was Dorica's ring. Perhaps it was a usual shape in Spain; I'd ask her on Saturday.

Or would I?

How could I possibly possess a tryptych that might have belonged in her mother's family?

I hauled myself from the chaise longue, rapidly dug out Uncle Ted's diaries from the baggage closet, and raced back to the terrace. He'd said his dearest friend had given it to him to keep for her, it came from Spain and she was dead. Suppose his diaries told who Elvira had married!

But when I'd finished deciphering his crabbed engi-

neer's handwriting, I was nowhere. Oh, it was James
Bond and the Man from UNCLE combined—even better because it was true—drily humorous reports of
robbing arsenals, fusing street lights while the six most
wanted Loyalists escaped, a fancy fracas in Ceuta; it
was all there except what I wanted.

Nowhere was a word of the triptych, nowhere a full
name of places or persons. Disappointedly, I riffled
through again—and sat up, concentrating: Arabic numbers for men who worked with him, Roman numerals
for important localities, a single initial for people or
places chance-met. There were XII places and 9 people
—*but not all at once.*

First, 1 and 2, in southern Spain; I to III were swiftly
finished and abandoned as he moved north from Madrid
and put together a cadre of daredevils: 3 to 7 appeared
swiftly, IV to VII, where the organization was completed. Thereafter, every number was on his own, re-
porting only to Uncle Ted: 1 and 6 were the receiving
end, 4 and 5 dispatched, 2 and 3 chaperoned convoys, 7
covered Uncle Ted personally . . . V and VI were finished, VIII to XI emerged, and finally there were 8 and
9 at XII, by which time the pace was frenetic.

The Rebs were hot on the trail, all the numbers were
working round the clock, and only XII and X were still
usable. 3 and 4 were sufficiently suspect that they'd been
replaced by 5 and 6, but it was Uncle Ted the Rebs
wanted, and the ace in his hole was that nobody knew
his real name!

In Spain, Theodore is Teodorico; the numbers called
him Rico, and most weren't sure of his last name. Patiently, the Rebels had picked up a word here and there,
until at last they were hunting for an American named
Rico Andes! Uncle Ted thought it one hell of a good

joke, because he'd spoken colloquial Mexican Spanish from childhood. He was fairly tall, with dark hair and eyes; he grew a luxuriant mustache; 2 got him a Mexican passport through a third cousin to explain the missing Castilian lisp, but shortly Uncle Ted could talk court Spanish, and 7 got him a Madrid identity card.

Three times he slid through Franco's fingers, but eventually he knew the game was up, he'd finish XII and make tracks. On the last page of the third diary was the final entry, marked "Xmas Eve, no space left but not needed; will remember forever, no man could ask more. Got clean away, 8 with me, unloaded the last, waited two hours with 9, but 7 made it. Says not finished yet, but think dare rest few nights, then scatter. No matter, now it's forever, I can wait."

Puzzled, I closed the book and pondered. No hint of romance? Suddenly, I realized these weren't personal diaries but file records—ledgers, listing what was smuggled for whom! The rest was only because he was still a kid, getting a kick out of adventure.

Frustrating to have only tiny clues: a rock slide swept a burro from the trail, snow and fog delayed a convoy, 5 lost his way but made the cave before daylight . . . Obviously mountains, the Pyrenees? XII was the crucial dispatch point; X was a stopover, and a long haul, but the only way after the Rebs nearly caught 3 at XI . . .

Somehow I knew 8 and 9 were women; 1 to 7 were in motion, 8 was always at XII with food and extra blankets . . . Elvira Revascues? The last night, Uncle Ted went ahead, leaving 7 to lock up.

Definitely, 7 was always the *fidus Achates,* so Rico Andes would have waited till hell froze—or gone back at the risk of his own life to rescue 7—but why should 8 have waited? *Only if I were of deep concern to her, also!* Who was 7? He must also be dead, and while Uncle Ted had learned of Elvira's death, had kept the triptych in memory of his friends, he must never have known there was a child—or I felt positive he'd have done something.

The diaries didn't disprove Dorica's legitimacy, but caution was strongly indicated—because if 7 had ever married 8, Uncle Ted would have said so. He'd mentioned when 4 became a father, he'd chuckled naughtily when 2 turned up safely in clothes borrowed from a barmaid acquaintance!

Luis Carvalhao, I thought with relief . . . although I had the impression he'd known Uncle Ted for only a short while in person, merely kept in touch by correspondence. Still, he might have a clue . . .

Hot sunshine illumined the gentle smile of Mary cuddling her Babe, and I shut the panels, thinking I'd set this in a dim corner of my future morning room with fresh flowers every day.

Flowers! I'd meant to coax myself to exercise by a walk to the florist. Now it was late afternoon, the hottest time—but I'd nothing else to do with Seb away. The silent apartment made me restless, no sign of Shadrach or Teresa. I found shade hat, purse, dark glasses . . .

An hour later, wringing wet from the sun, I stepped gratefully onto the entrance tiles. "Mad dogs and Englishmen!" Removing the sun glasses, I could see the wicker basket of flowers sitting in the upper hall. Odd. Where was Teresa? Involuntarily I turned to the lower apartment, tried the knob, and the door swung open.

"Teresa?" Might as well inspect those draperies. I tilted a blind, and there was no doubt they needed renewing. The lining was in rags, the heavy silk slitting at a touch. Carefully I set the panel down and looked about curiously: essence of 1925 Main Street, cluttered, fussy, ornate, hideous! My eyes moved around the room—and stopped.

On the farthest table stood my triptych, panels opened, and before it, a superb chalice of intricate gold wire enclosing glowing ruby glass. Incredulously, I examined it, but I had no real doubt. Here was the mate to Uncle Ted's triptych, complete even to the diamond-shaped ring. Gently I picked up the chalice, admiring the deep color of the cup held in a metal framework at once so sturdy yet so fanciful and airy. If only I could find something similar—but I'd never be able to display my triptych, I realized suddenly!

How could I explain, without adding to Dorica's bastardy by implication? One point was settled: Uncle Ted had known Elvira. How long had the triptych been sitting here? Perhaps ever since Señora Revascues's death, and no one had known it should have gone to Doutor Silva along with Dorica.

Teresa would know. I reclosed the blinds to protect the faded colors and went in search of her. "Teresa?" She must be in the kitchen; I could feel fresh air, probably the garden door opened. Halfway along the hall, I heard masculine voices behind me.

Instinctively I faded into the shadows, my heart pounding. Of all disasters, to be caught here in the apartment of a woman who didn't recognize my existence! A solid American voice was saying, "Sorry to inconvenience you, Mr. Revascues, but I've got to leave tonight instead of tomorrow."

"*Por nada,* Mr. Kupperman; my pleasure, I assure you, for you will truly appreciate our chalice."

I stood spellbound. *Miguel Revascues?* He was continuing smoothly, "One of a pair, made about 1250 for the Revascues twins who originally possessed the triptychs—for there was once a mate for it, too."

"Beautiful!" Kupperman's voice was reverent, yearning.

"The triptych is not for sale, not at any price."

"I don't blame you, but tell me about it, anyway."

"There were two, done by Brother Ambrose for Miguel and Juan Revascues who studied at the University of Salamanca, and there were two chalices to stand before the triptychs, but one of each was lost during the Spanish Civil War."

"So this is unique? All right, how much?"

"Five thousand."

There was a long silence, a nervous flick of a cigarette lighter, but I knew Mr. Kupperman was a gone goose. So did my unknown brother-in-law. "Taxes, loss on exchange," he murmured, "but in a private transaction there is no publicity. We both know the chalice would bring more at Sotheby's . . ."

"Okay," Kupperman capitulated. There were faint sounds of opening a checkbook, pen scratches, "Zurich, as usual? What's that number again?"

"24226." The numbers made a pattern: two, then forty-two for Seb and twenty-six for me. "If you ever decide to sell the triptych, I'll give you fifty thousand, Mr. Revascues."

"A generous offer, thank you—but it is enough to be forced to part with the chalice," Miguel sighed. "Eye surgery is ruinously expensive, but for my wife, only the best will do."

I stood, startled in the dimness; did Seb know Branca needed an operation? Kupperman was heavily tactful, "Sorry it's needed again. I hope this time does it for her."

He was receding, asking, "Any luck on that goblet, incidentally?"

"I think I know where it is . . . private hands," Miguel's voice was a shrug, "and a family that does not need money."

"Damn," Kupperman muttered. "I'll go three thousand to complete the set. See what can be done, will you, Revascues?"

"Of course. A pleasure to see you again after so long . . ." Sounds of parting, a door firmly closed. But Miguel was still there, whistling with soft satisfaction . . . and I remembered Teresa's stubborn insistence that no one used the apartment, "I would know, Dona . . ."

She'd know by a cigarette stub, a soiled ashtray . . .

I fled backwards to the kitchen, jarring a table in the dark hall and hearing rapid footsteps, but I was across the garden to the shrubs overgrown at the bottom of our terrace steps, cowering motionless, shielding my face and thanking heaven I'd worn a dark dress. Peering cautiously through the oleanders, I saw a small man reconnoitering at the kitchen door, and beside me a familiar voice said, "Mrrrrow?"

So this was Shadrach's siesta spot? He clambered onto my knees, purring throatily, and Miguel retreated, softly closing the door. I supposed he was washing and drying Kupperman's ashtray, but with the cat's weight on my lap and cool shadows about me, I sat still to steady my breathing—and suddenly the door reopened stealthily. "Pssssss, pssssss, m'nou, m'nou . . ."

I pinched Shadrach's tail sharply, producing an indignant "mrrrAWWWW!" and Miguel was apparently satisfied. He drew the door shut once more, and I could hear the soft click of the latch. I continued to sit possum-still for uncounted minutes.

Why did Miguel Revascues fear human witness to his sale?

Because the chalice he'd so touchingly sold Mr. Kupperman was a fake!

chapter 6

Was there any other answer?

I lay limply in the lounge chair, closing my eyes, but the mind was a whirling dervish. I'd understood Miguel Revascues was ruined by the war, had a made-job of managing Carranca to give him walking-around money, and I'd just heard him pocket a check for five grand to a Swiss numbered account. Did Seb know of his brother-in-law's lucrative sideline? Of course not! Even Teresa didn't know anyone was ever in that apartment, not in seven years.

She was in the kitchen now, placidly preparing for dinner. She had already arranged the flowers for the table when she returned from her siesta. I lit a cigarette and concentrated.

Kupperman was a long-time client, but hadn't been here in some time—I'd heard occasional motion downstairs in the weeks before I married Seb, so there must be other clients, who came in the evening, after Teresa would be gone. That figured: Miguel had no fear of a tenant or visiting fireman. If caught, he was a family member, dropping by to look at the apartment, and until today, he hadn't been caught for seven years. He'd chanced this afternoon; greed and an important client outweighed caution. Besides, by all standards of Lisbon aristocracy I should have been lolling at a beach club, while my maid napped on the top floor, out of earshot and behind drawn blinds.

Was the secrecy only to conceal Miguel's hidden business from Seb? Perhaps. I'd a hunch Swiss numbered accounts required a minimum five figure balance, and Seb wouldn't be happy to know his penniless brother-in-law possessed one!

Why did I think the chalice a fake? Oh, elementary, my dear Watson! Miguel had said the mates to triptych and chalice were lost during the war—but I had the triptych. I'd also have the chalice, if there ever was one. Even if the glass were broken, the gold framework could stand alone and would have been preserved.

No, the chalice did not accompany the triptych. It might still be genuine, a commission sale from someone avoiding publicity. Surely, at these prices, Kupperman would have an independent appraisal—or would he? He might rely on Miguel's integrity, although I'd never heard Miguel was an art expert.

But his wife was.

Was Branca a partner, using her remaining eyesight and trained knowledge to assist her husband? Reason said Miguel couldn't possibly have been selling art forgeries for seven years without a dust-up sometime! A man who will pay five thousand for a bit of glass set in gold wire is not about to be fooled so easily.

The alternative was that the chalice was genuine—and

Miguel either had no right to sell it or wished no witness to the price he'd received. Good heavens, was Seb's brother-in-law a *fence?*

At dinner, "Teresa, if you have the key, I'll look at the draperies tonight."

"*Sim, sim,* I have keys, but how will you see?"

"Well enough to know if they must be replaced."

It took two keys to open the front door—and one glance to see there was nothing on the corner table but a lamp and a clean ashtray. Dutifully inspecting rotten fabrics, I admired his cleverness. How many times had he bemused a wealthy collector by the genuine triptych, implying authentication of what he was selling?

"You are right, I must look in daylight," I told Teresa. "Give me the keys, I'll come tomorrow." She handed them over unhesitatingly, although I wasn't sure what I'd do with a duplicate set, once I had them made. I toyed with actually getting new draperies; imagine Miguel's shock, next time he opened the door, to find his hidey-hole redecorated! Enjoyable to contemplate, but not practical, until I knew a bit more.

The major problem was Seb: I ought to be able to dump this in his lap, but that would lead to Elvira's triptych and Dorica, to say nothing of the chance that Branca was involved. I thought drily that there was a sardonic righteous retribution about it— It was the triptych that had led to Uncle Ted's diaries, that had detained me, so that I'd returned when I should have been at the beach or lying on the terrace . . . whereby I'd seen the other triptych. I'd been through the diaries three times; try once more?

Under the strong study lamp, I went word by word, page by page, ending with a few tiny possibilities: A shipment mid-1938 included AR, 7 in charge—Annunciata Revascues? One reference I had missed before: "7, carita and I reached XII safely," after transferring a convoy to 3. Early December I found carita again—insisting on wax candles "to be lighted at the moment," although shipping space was scant—but 7 strapped the package to his back.

Still unsettled whether Elvira was 8 or only a passenger, still no hint of a wedding. Dorica was my age, meaning born in 1939 . . . but perhaps conceived in January, after the diaries ended, when Uncle Ted was gone and the numbers scattered to safety? For the first time I wondered whether I had all his diaries. Might there be more, buried in our Salem barn? It seemed strange he wouldn't have recorded his adventures with the Maquis, later with the OSS. One hell of a job to go through everything, but when Seb and I went home, I would do it! Meanwhile, I wrapped diaries and triptych in a ski sweater, in my bottom bureau drawer.

Lisbon had learned Seb was away. "Persis, *querida,* what is this loneliness? Come to lunch—dinner—we insist!" Dutifully I accepted, only to miss two phone calls from Seb. "Didn't you *tell* him where I was?" I asked Teresa, anguished.

"*Sim, sim,*" she nodded, "but he says he will not disturb your pleasure, to say only that he called and returns Monday."

"Thank you, Teresa." Controlling myself, I finished making up while she fussed about—until I knew there was something on her mind. In the mirror I could see her nerving herself, her face scared to death, her hands twisting together. "What is it, Teresa?" I asked quietly. "You can tell me anything."

To my surprise, she nodded and took a few steps toward me. "It is true—you are a witch?" she whispered.

Startled, I met her eyes in the mirror, my mouth open to say, "Of course not, that was only Dom Sebastiao's nonsense." Her expression stopped me.

Teresa WANTED me to be a witch.

Good heavens, what to say? I gulped, and sighted the miniature. "Come here, Teresa." I picked it up. "No, I am not a witch, it was only a joke. See, here is a picture of my very-great-grandmother who was supposed to be a witch."

She crept forward, peering. "That is the witch?"

"I'm afraid she wasn't either, Teresa. People just said she was. I'm sorry." Why on earth was it so important, but I knew it was. She was gazing at Old Persis almost hungrily.

"Where did this witch live, Dona? What was she called?"

"She lived in America hundreds of years ago, and her name was Persis, too, but she wasn't really a witch, Teresa. That was only Dom Sebastiao's joke, believe me!"

"America, aaah!" Teresa sighed with satisfaction, looking at me in the mirror. *"Sim, sim,* the eyes are the same, the name—even, there is a cat."

As if on cue, Shadrach leapt to the edge of the dressing table, sniffing delicately and bending to kiss my nose; he is partial to Magie—but nothing could have been worse timed, quite apart from the name of his favorite perfume! I knew by Teresa's face that I'd never disillusion her, but why was she so happy? "Aren't you afraid to work for a witch?"

"Sim, sim, but you are different. Eh, I should have

known," she shook her head ruefully, "but I grow old and forgetful."

"What are you talking about?" I was half-alarmed by her glee. What did she expect me to do, change snails into rubies or something? "You must believe me: I am NOT a witch!"

It was useless. Dom Sebastiao had said I was a witch, a witch I was—and I'd only innocently made things worse by trying to explain Old Persis. One crumb of comfort: apparently I was a good witch, highly desirable to have in the family. Teresa was wreathed in smiles, almost skipping, assuring me, "Eh, I say nothing, never fear! You will arrange all to suit yourself when the time comes." At the door, she curtsied respectfully, and then she was gone. I stared after her in growing fury.

Dammit, this was too much. On top of all my other problems, I was going to have to be a witch because of Seb's joke? If I could have got my hands on Sebastiao dos Martim, I'd have forgotten whether or no he loved me, whether or no his brother-in-law was involved in shady art dealings with his wife's connivance and secreting the profits in Switzerland—and I'd have smacked my husband with all the force of a strong right arm trained at Radcliffe to wield a hockey stick.

All the way to the dinner party I fumed inwardly, but with an undercurrent of uneasiness. What was the significance of a blue-eyed witch that made Teresa so happy? Abandoning the car to the attendant, I went forward—and stopped dead in sudden realization. It concerned the Carranca Curse, of course. I might not know how, nor had I thought Seb so credulous—*but the fact remained that he'd known of Old Persis before he proposed.*

Dorica willingly told me all she knew, which added up to zero. Señora Revascues simply turned up one day late in October 1939 with a baby girl she said was her granddaughter. Teresa assumed she'd been sent by the family; Doutor Silva assumed the child legitimate.

"Why not? She gave my name and birthdate, said my mother died of pneumonia and my father was at war. Doutor Silva asked no questions—if only he had! Afterward, it turned out no one had the faintest idea she was here! Branca and Dona Benedecta were caught in Greece, got across to Turkey and stayed; Sebastiao was in England, Miguel in Madrid. He admits he knew Agueda Grande was empty but assumed the women had got through the mountains to Carranca."

"Mountains?"

"The Serra da Estrella," she nodded, "rugged as the Alps, but only about fifty miles from Agueda Grande to Carranca. When everyone got home in 1945, grandmother was dead, I was living with Doutor Silva, who'd thought it was only a matter of turning me over to a family member." Dorica smiled faintly. "Miguel flatly refused without 'wedding lines.' We tried—but no luck."

"Why d'you think Elvira was married?" I asked uneasily, because Dorica's birthday was August 15, 1939, meaning Uncle Ted would have known—unless the ceremony was only when necessary.

"Grandmother described the wedding," Dorica said. "Doutor Silva admitted at the end, she did ramble, but there were details, Persis: the branched candlesticks from the banquet hall—Father Juan brought a Christmas rose—sad to marry without a veil, but for a hundred candles, the Virgin would surely send happiness.

"It *happened*," Dorica stated, "but not at Agueda

Grande. The priest was Father Juan, but he swore he'd never married Elvira to anyone. He knew she loved someone working dangerously; she'd never mentioned the name. When she and grandmother vanished, he wasn't surprised; he knew there were Portuguese relatives—and after the fall of Gijon, Franco forces moved south as well as north, wiping out resistance pockets while the main fighting was at Teruel. There were only the two women alone, known to be staunch Loyalists," she shrugged. "Only much later that anyone knew Miguel was actually fighting for Franco."

"He was a *Rebel?*"

"And very important, sent here and there as special envoy, while Franco was welching on his commitments," Dorica snorted with satisfaction, "but when he got home, he found Agueda Grande stripped! Everything! Paintings, silver, furniture, even the rugs."

"What happened to the things?" I knew the answer.

Dorica grinned wickedly. "Years later one of the Goyas turned up in a private auction; Miguel made a fuss, but there was a bill of sale signed by both Elvira and Annunciata Revascues. Presumably, that's the way everything went."

"I see—except I don't. Where's the money?"

"Nobody knows. She got ten thousand for the Goya, there were three others, plus two El Grecos and a Velasquez. I haven't an inventory, but from Miguel's rage— he said my mother was a *thief!*—we suspect she realized several hundred thousand, but grandmother didn't have it, Persis. There was only about a thousand dollars when she died, and Teresa was positive she'd sold jewelry before she became really ill."

"What became of your father, who was he?"

"I've no idea," she said helplessly. "I don't know

where I was born; Doutor Silva and Teresa had to make depositions so I could get a passport. There wasn't one scrap of paper, not even an old letter. Once grandmother said I looked like my mother but had 'Peo's' hands—and near the end of 1939 she said she'd heard my father had been killed in Belgium. She was terribly sad, but she never told Doutor Silva any facts.

"I suppose she never thought they'd be needed, so I have the unique honor of being the Revascues bastard," Dorica finished, leaning forward to pick up her drink. Unconsciously I glanced at her hand, curled about the glass. The fingers were slender and graceful, but the middle finger was disproportionately long, the pinky was oddly short and bent askew at the tip.

For a second I thought I might be going to faint, because I knew that hand.

It was Uncle Ted's.

Somehow I got through the evening. Afterwards I sat on the terrace in a state of shock.

The doctor had misunderstood, of course. It was not Peo, but *Teo,* and Dorica was not only my third cousin by marriage but my second cousin by blood—and she was illegitimate, no matter what Annunciata Revascues had muttered on her deathbed. Sickly, I thought everything pointed to a wartime *affaire;* they'd meant to marry—it was their *plans* Señora Revascues described as fact. Uncle Ted had not died in Belgium, and to the best of anyone's knowledge, he'd never married. Certainly he'd have told daddy; they were very close despite different fathers.

Wartime, uncertain communication—he'd known Elvira was dead, didn't know there was a child that might be his. And thinking him dead, Señora Revascues had shielded her daughter as best she could. That was why there were no papers, why she'd dropped no usable words to Doutor Silva.

What to do? Ethically, my inheritance belonged to Dorica, but how could I transfer it? Miguel might love me forever for confirming illegitimacy; his affection was the last thing I wanted. Write daddy the whole story, I decided; ask him to hunt in the barn for anything that might give a clue to the numbers. Ask Luis Carvalhao for any tidbit Uncle Ted might have let fall.

Shadrach leapt softly into my lap, I stroked him absently, tremulously. What had I got myself into? Renée had said I'd married in haste, should have known more about Sebastiao—but, dismally honest, I knew I'd have married him no matter what. With a sigh, I stubbed my cigarette, picked up Shadrach, said "To bed!"

He purred his best, but he was no substitute for Sebastiao.

chapter 7

Sebastiao came home.

It was always a minor marvel that so tall a man could move so silently. I was leaning on the terrace wall, watching Shadrach stalk a bird who was perfectly aware of his presence. Just as the cat sprang, the bird flitted to the mimosa tree, where it swayed, telling Shadrach he'd made a fool of himself. "Silly! Birds are for singing, why d'you think I put a bell on you," I advised him affectionately——and felt accustomed arms.

"Silly, yourself! Wives are for kissing, why d'you think I put a ring on you, *queridinho?*" Seb laughed softly in my ear. With a cry, I swiveled to raise my lips. *"Por deus,"* he muttered after a moment, "it is worth going away if one returns to such a welcome. You are happy to see me, *minha mulher?*"

"Yes!"

"You have missed me, longed for me?"

"I have missed you every minute of every day, longed for you every second of every night."

"Even while dining with friends? You could not keep your mind on the conversation for missing me? What a stimulating guest you must have been!" he teased.

"Oh, everyone understood," I assured him. "That was why they asked me: so I could miss you in public." I burrowed against him happily. "Mmmmm, I didn't expect you until tomorrow."

"Nor I, but Luis can finish, and this morning . . ."

"You suddenly recalled a wife, you drove like the wind, and arrived in time for dinner!"

Seb laughed. "Where is Teresa?"

"I gave her the day off."

"Ah? Then let me change clothes and we will go to the club. Do you object to telephone we are coming, *querida?*"

"No—but do you object to staying home?" I asked tentatively. "There's a chicken and things, or are you too hungry to wait?"

"You—would cook for me?" he said after a moment.

"More trouble to dress and go out. Wouldn't you love a cool shower and comfortable slacks," I suggested seductively, "drinks on the terrace, prop your feet up instead of stepping on brakes?"

"How can I resist? I have long suspected that serpent in the Garden of Eden was a female . . ."

That was the happiest evening. I thought, hopefully, it seemed almost planned: the two of us alone, Seb replete with a good dinner and relaxing . . . surely he'd be receptive to his wife's puzzlements?

First, the food. I went back and forth, "How hungry are you? Shall we have asparagus, or risotto and salad?" I fixed a highball, yelled into the shower, "Drink on the bureau!" I was basting the chicken with Vermouth and melted butter when I found Seb, drink in hand, a most peculiar expression on his face.

"You are singing," he said curiously. "It makes you happy to do a servant's work?"

"This is no servant's work, it's creative art! Fix me a drink, please?"

By dinner's end I had a new perspective on Seb. He ate with evident relish and fulsome praise; he talked more explicitly of the business in Oporto than usual. He laughed heartily at my recital of Lisbon gossip. Over the dinner table, we were close and intimate, husband and wife alone together—but while I scraped and stacked dishes for Teresa, I sensed a sort of bewilderment in Seb, lounging on the terrace. I suddenly knew that what seemed entirely normal to me was unknown to him: that a wife should cook, a husband should carry a tray. From what I knew of Cristinha and Dona Benedecta, neither would ever have got him so much as a glass of water, let alone a meal. He'd never experienced small domestic intimacies, knew nothing of partnership at home, or sharing anything aside from a bed.

He still reacted like any other man to a good home-cooked dinner. In a surge of optimism, I thought cockily, *I'll teach you a new way of life, my lad!* Wiping my hands, I switched off the kitchen light and sallied forth to await the strategic moment—not certain what I meant to say, yet positive tonight would settle something between us . . .

Shadrach found the zircon.

He dragged it up to the terrace and dropped it at my feet with a commanding "MrrraowwWW," just as Seb extended a glass of Benedictine. Instinctively, he bent to pick it up, while I peered curiously, "What's he got?"

Sebastiao straightened to his full height. "I threw away this piece of trash once, why does it return?" Disdainfully, he extended the ring, and after a month of exposure, it was nearly unrecognizable—the setting twisted, the stone filthy. Seb's face was equally twisted, ugly.

"I—don't know," I faltered, while Shadrach leapt onto the foot of my lounge and reared on his hind legs, pawing at the ring and growling urgently. "I think he thinks it's his, maybe he wants it on his collar again."

"Your cat has little discrimination," Seb remarked harshly, "and less excuse. It does not match *his* eyes."

"I don't suppose he knows that, he's just used to having it . . ."

"Shadrach is accustomed to jewels? I'll get him a diamond collar."

"Don't be absurd, of course he isn't used to jewels."

"I'll get him something to match *his* eyes," Seb repeated, glaring at the zircon. "*This* goes into the garbage, you understand?"

"Of course," I nodded, half-frightened by his furious contempt. He strode away, I saw him bending over the kitchen trash, then he was back—but the peaceful mood was gone. We spoke to each other conventionally for the rest of the evening, and finally went to bed, where felicity returned.

In the darkness, when my breathing had steadied, I was nerved enough to murmur, "Seb—could I talk to you, please?"

The answer was a faint snore.

I could almost have thought Seb was jealous, but when he produced a custom-made red leather collar that was hung not only with bell and name tag for Shadrach dos Martim, but sported an immense yellow Brazilian diamond as well, I knew it was only that even Seb's cat must be elegant, above Greenwich Village jewelry. Shadrach was sinfully proud of his collar. He went down to visit Dorica, although how did he know she was at home that day? She telephoned, "Shadrach has come to see me, what d'you think of *that?*"

"Not much," I returned. "He only wants to show off the collar Seb gave him. What a pair of snobs!"

Looking at Shadrach strutting across the terrace later, I could have hit him for ruining the only approach to real intimacy I'd ever achieved. Once lost, it never returned. We were back to the old politeness, "The Perutas want us for a beach party," or *"Querida,* you will like to join the Limons at the club?"

"If you only knew what you did," I said despairingly, picking him up with a slight shake. "I was so close, and you fouled me up."

"Hrmmmph!" Shadrach snorted briefly, struggling from my arms. Teresa was in the kitchen.

I'd spent a full day outlining the situation for daddy before Seb got home, but a letter from mummy crossed mine; they were going to Maine for three weeks, so I couldn't hope for an immediate answer at that end. I'd heard no further sounds below. I returned Teresa's keys, *"Obrigado,"* and with my own, I prowled through the apartment, finding nothing but a wall safe behind a bedroom picture. Even if Teresa knew the combination, what excuse could I give for wanting to open?

With Seb home, I had to suppress all consideration of the puzzle; he noticed in twenty-four hours. "What is this absence of mind, Persis? There is something troubling you?"

It should have been the perfect opening, but his voice was impatient. "Sorry, I was only wondering if they'd got the tiles into the right bathrooms," I fibbed hastily, but he wasn't fooled.

He looked at me sharply. "That is why you are listening so intently? You expect to *hear* the tile setter making a mistake?"

"No, of course not, but it is rather on my mind."

"Abandon it, if you please, and allow me to be on your mind instead. For the third time, *querida:* shall we go sailing with the Henriques tomorrow?"

"That would be delightful . . ."

I told myself Miguel Revascues was not my concern; let Seb find out on his own. Now the first shock was past, I half-forgot Dorica. I might know she was my cousin, but until I could prove legitimacy, it must remain a secret.

The tiles were set, the house beginning to take shape. I came home one afternoon to find Luis Carvalhao on the terrace. "Seb is caught at the warehouse, Renée is lunching with an old friend," he glanced at his watch, his eyes twinkling. "Four o'clock already—but it is a very old friend!"

"Evidently—but good to see you alone, Luis."

"Equally good to see you, Persis," he said, quietly. "All goes well?"

I sat silent for a moment. "Yes, and no—but mostly yes, and I expect the no is only a matter of adjustment. Luis," I looked at him directly, "did you ever hear the name Rico Andes?"

His face went white, and he sat up slowly. "Where did you hear it?"

"Uncle Ted's diaries."

"He—*wrote?* My God, Persis, it may be twenty-five years, but not everyone is dead."

"He doesn't identify anyone, Luis." I was rocked by the intensity of his reaction, but I must know. "Luis—*who was 8?*"

The shock technique didn't work. "Eight?" he echoed, blankly. "What are you talking about, Persis?"

"He used numbers for people, Roman numerals for localities. There were seven men and two women," unconsciously, I lowered my voice, *willing* him to tell me. Useless. Luis didn't know!

"Persis, you don't realize!" he muttered nervously. "There are scores to settle purely for revenge. No one must know you are related, or you might be in danger, too! Never mention his name, you understand!" He was shaken, horrified. "Seven men and two women?" he said under his breath. "My God, I never knew there were so many—and I do not want to know anything more, Persis!"

"Then I won't tell you," I soothed, "but there's something else, that has to be proved another way, but I *must* know whatever you know, Luis."

"The less you know, the better—believe me, Persis!"

"It has to do with my family, but unless I can piece together a few more facts in that particular period, I can't settle the matter," I said carefully. "You see, I always knew he was a political smuggler with a price on his head, but until now I'd thought you were only casual friends. Where did you meet, Luis?"

"In Ceuta," he said reluctantly. "His job was ended, we went to Madrid on holiday. The war began, and he suggested we could help refugees because of our foreign passports. For a while we were there with—someone else. Then I went to Oporto, and I never saw him again."

His voice trailed away, but already I knew Luis was 1, "someone else" was 2.

"He went north, organized an escape route through the Serra da Estrella . . . what was your job, Luis?"

"Passports, sending people on coastal cargo boats to Lisbon, holding cash until claimed," he admitted.

"Was all of it claimed?" I asked quickly, but he only nodded. "Did you know the man in Lisbon?" It *had* to be 6 . . .

"No. None of us ever knew more than one other person, and Rico, of course. We couldn't slip, even if caught; he was the only one who knew everything, that's why he was vital to the Rebs. Towards the end, there were trips every night; not one was ever caught. He saved hundreds of people *and* their valuables," Luis looked at me compellingly. "Nearly a million dollars passed through my hands alone. Now d'you understand, Persis? He hurt Franco more than the Abraham Lincoln Brigade."

"I'll bet!" I murmured, awed. If Luis had had that much, 6 must have had even more. Did he still have Elvira's cash, unclaimed? "If you never knew anyone, how did you keep in touch, Luis?"

He smiled. "Any peasant anywhere would help 'Rico.' Somehow he got them food or medicine, a priest or a doctor. So—a note, hand to hand, market to market, *comprendido?* The last was New Year's Eve: he was safe, all was finished. Then two weeks later, F . . ." he cleared his throat, "someone else sent word he'd been traced. He got to Oporto, wouldn't meet me for fear I'd be identified. We got him to Bordeaux; someone else and I carried on for a couple of months, until there was nothing more to do.

"Then we got the usual grimy note: already, two

attempts. So we arranged for a body to be identified by six different peasants as Rico Andes," Luis finished simply. "He moved about enough to lose the trail, but just as he thought it might be safe to try for home, the European war began. You know the rest."

"Yes." I sat back, discouraged. Nothing, except that Señora Revascues had believed the false death story, had never tried to tell Uncle Ted he had a daughter—and, knowing Elvira was dead, Uncle Ted never tried to reach her mother. Teresa was bringing out the drink tray. I said, as though changing the subject, "Did you ever know Elvira Revascues?"

"Who?" Luis looked blank. "Oh, Miguel's sister with the illegitimate child," he identified and got up to prepare drinks. "No, of course not. They were Rebs," he said contemptuously. But of course it was only Miguel who'd backed Franco, never Elvira . . . so that was another dead end, and the only hope was finding another diary in the files at Salem.

"Have you told anyone else?" Luis was asking, urgently. He sighed with relief when I shook my head. "Don't! Not even Seb, you understand, Persis? I beg of you, burn the diaries! Forget you ever read them, never mention his name."

"Seb already knows I had an Uncle Ted," I said, uneasily.

"Who died years ago, whom you never knew very well! For your own sake, Persis, let it go at that!" Luis was still shaken, tossing off a straight shot of brandy. "Even I," he said in a low voice, "even now . . . you understand?"

I nodded. "One last question: who was his personal aide-de-camp? You must have known, or guessed." I held my breath. If only I could find 7—and already I could see Teresa opening the door for Renée.

"I suspected Jaime d'Artois," Luis muttered, "but we'll never know. He was killed in Belgium, working with the Underground . . . ah, Renée *minha coraçao,* at last you are finished with this interminable luncheon?"

That was that, and Luis was no help, aside from impressing me with the danger of what little I knew. Next day I packed the diaries and phoned Pedro Silva. "Would you ask Dorica to take some family papers to New York? I'd feel safer if they were mailed stateside." I debated sending the triptych, but I might need it if this thing boiled over—and I could always say I'd bought it on Third Avenue.

Two days later, Seb found me finishing a letter to my sister. *"Querida,"* he kissed my neck, "how do you endure this miserable object when you demand an electric machine in my office?"

"Now I'm married to you, I must be economical!"

Seb laughed, picking up the battered dictionary and lounging against the desk, turning pages idly. "Where did you get this?"

"It was Uncle Ted's, I used it in college. Spelling is not one of my talents," I said absently, typing the final lines.

He tossed it back to the desk. "One sees you have constant need of it. Buy a new one, *querida;* the edition is too old."

"I suppose—although so far I don't seem to want to spell any new words." I addressed an envelope, inserted my letter, closed with a thump. "Toss me the stamp box, sweetie?"

"Tell me of this Edward Bradbury of whom you were so fond."

"*Who?*"

"Your Uncle Ted."

I had an inexplicable throb of caution. "Nothing to tell, darling. He was my godfather, he had a ranch in Texas and was killed at a rodeo." I set the stamp in place and rose, smiling. "Drink time! The Limons will be here any moment . . ."

I stole back later. On the flyleaf was *Theodore Anderson.* Automatically I ripped out the page and flushed the scraps down the loo. But what did the name mean to Seb that he'd deliberately set a trap for me? He was looking at that page as he asked about Edward Bradbury, and re-membering Luis's warning, I'd lied by failing to say, "It was Ted for Theodore."

Yet, how could Seb know of Rico Andes, when he was only a schoolboy in England? He was no backer of Franco, even today. Why hadn't I told the truth? Seb could be no threat to any of the numbers, if Luis didn't know who they were.

Next day I ripped the dictionary apart, stuffed the pieces into separate trash cans of decorators' waste around our house, and bought a new collegiate. From the terrace I saw Seb enter the study. He came out so quickly I knew he'd only verified the change, but he said nothing at first. We were finishing a drink, "I see you bought a new dictionary."

"Your word is law! Now I shall spell astronaut prop-erly."

He smiled absently. *"Querida,* I do not wish to pry into your secrets—but if they should concern me, also?" His voice was softly reflective. I was as hypnotized as a rabbit by a stoat, and the telephone rang.

Saved by Alexander Graham, I sighed thankfully, but Seb was already coming back. I rose, as if ready to go. "Finish the drink, *meu amor,* we are late."

He ignored me, refilling our glasses. "Why did you discard the dictionary?"

"You told me to get a new one."

"But you have not really discarded, have you? Merely hidden among your treasures. Where do you keep them, I wonder? A pity the zircon is missing!" He tossed off a straight shot and thumped the glass on the table, while I stood flabbergasted. "How often do you take them out, to remember these Arties and Teddies? You think quickly, *minha mulher!* You recall the name—but you cannot turn Edward Bradbury into Theodore Anderson," he snarled, catching my shoulders brutally. *"Who was he?"*

I was completely caught off base. Was it some sort of new trap, or did Seb really think him an old boy friend—but if so, why such rage? "He wasn't anybody. When I went to college, I took the dictionary from my uncle's books," I stammered. "I never looked at the flyleaf. Perhaps he got it secondhand."

"Ah, you keep your secrets well!" Seb let me go with such suddenness that I staggered against the iron lounge frame, while he straightened his cuffs contemptuously. I was conscious of sheer fury. Damn his arrogance!

"I have no such 'secrets' as you imply, and if you recall our wedding night, the defense rests," I remarked, and swept on before he could speak. "If I can ignore the women you've slept with all over the world in the past twenty-five years—because you needn't try to tell me you were ever faithful to Cristinha, and very possibly you aren't faithful to me, either," I stated, coldly, "you will damn well accept the fact that a few other men may have taken me to dances or sent flowers. I wasn't the girl nobody wanted—or did you think you did me a favor to marry me?"

I picked up my glass and gulped with bravado, while Seb silently looked at the terrazzo tiles. "You are right, why should I expect more than I have to give," he muttered, putting his arms about me and stroking my hair. "You gave me everything, I know it. Why should you not have had your share of arms and kisses?" His arm tightened convulsively, relaxed. "The wife of dos Martim must be his alone, but so you are, *minha coraçao,* and I should be eternally humble to have found you." He laid his cheek against my temple with a sigh. "We can forget this, I can be pardoned?"

"Yes," I said shakily, "but it's a bit much if you're going to fuss over every little boy who carried my books to school."

"I can see this would take all my time," he agreed. "I must adjust myself to ignoring everything in your life before you mistook me for the night watchman." I giggled helplessly, and Seb let me go with a hug. "Get your wrap, *querida,* we are really late."

"Your fault, you think up the excuse!" I dashed for scarf and purse, dashed back to Seb at the open door.

"I have the excuse," he announced, whisking me into the car. "I shall say, 'Congratulate me, at last I am really a married man. We are late because my wife and I were having a fight.' What do you think of that?"

"Not too highly."

"Ah? What is wrong with it?"

"It's inconclusive. As an American woman, I must tell you it is imperative to leave no doubt as to who won."

"Then I say all was my fault, I am a jealous old man?" He stretched out a hand, smiling.

"Hah! Who'd believe that of dos Martim?"

"Por fim, a man who has a beautiful wife needs no excuse at all," he chuckled. "I murmur apologies to the hostess, raise an eyebrow to the host, throw out my chest, sigh with satisfaction—and all will explain itself."

"Seb, you *wouldn't!"*

"Why not? We have not been married long. In fact," he said, judicially, "we will need no excuses for at least a year."

"And after that?" I asked, straight-faced.

He drew in to the curb and eyed me. "For you, that excuse will serve forever," he said softly, tilting my chin to kiss me. "Persis, my blue-eyed witch!"

I drew back sharply. "Why d'you say that, what does it mean, Seb? You know I'm not a witch . . ."

"Are you not? But you have bewitched me, *queri-dinho!"* With a laugh, he was already out of the driver's seat, while the car boy stood behind me. The host was throwing wide the entrance, jovial and welcoming, hastening forward to embrace Seb heartily.

Slowly, I climbed from the car, mentally kicking myself. Why was I such a coward, why couldn't I lay it on the line, say "Sit down, I wish to talk to you!" And why had he tried a second, more subtle trap for "Theodore Anderson"? Had I succeeded in convincing him I knew nothing? I thought desperately that I had too many other people to protect by silence. Moving forward beside my husband, watching his tall figure bending gracefully over a feminine hand, I knew with devastating honesty that the only person I wished to protect was myself.

Face it: I would be deaf, dumb and blind, in order to keep this man to whom I was only another possession.

chapter 8

"Can you be ready to leave for Carranca tomorrow morning?"

"Yes." I felt startled. "For how long? Is Duarte coming back with us?"

"No. We will stay a few days."

I wanted to ask what sort of clothes to pack, but Seb's face was NO. "What time do you want to start?"

"After breakfast, we'll lunch in Coimbra."

The day began badly with a minor business crisis that delayed us an hour. Seb was taciturn and unsmiling, driving to an inch while I tried not to look. Now that I faced meeting his family, I was a bundle of nerves. How would I be received, would they like me, what should I do or say? I'd nothing to guide me beyond a few unguarded comments from Renée and the other Lisbon women: the house was gloomy, the food good, there were ski parties until Caterina dos Passos was killed.

Was she the X-factor that had kept Seb single? No, or it would be the apartment he wished redecorated rather than the house. Was my husband capable of love at all? Each Wednesday there was a letter from Duarte, being tutored by the parish priest and an Englishman, Mr. Wilson. Occasionally Seb's face softened over these letters—but did he love his son, who never came to visit?

Rushing toward Coimbra, I felt close to tears. It was too soon, before I was ready—yet how would it have been better a month hence? By Seb's expression, he had no more taste for this trip than I. Was the unscheduled visit to force recognition of a new wife by unheralded arrival?

After a lunch of which Seb ate little more than I, we started again. Buckled into the seat of the Ghia, I sat silent, my mind a hash of random fears, until I decided, "I'm damned sick of playing everything by ear. I'm not a rabbit, I'm a wife, even if not the sort he's used to."

So let him learn, I thought coldly. *There's no future to this.* I sat up briskly, conscious of chilly air. We were in a desolate world of mountains obscuring sun. I pulled the fur stole from the rear seat and rolled up my window.

"I should have warned you of the sharp temperature change," Seb apologized, reaching to the heater control. "Are you comfortable?"

"Quite, thanks. Would you like a cigarette?"

"If you please." Unsmiling, he held his eyes on the winding road while I lit up, said "Open!" and stuck the cigarette in his mouth. He smoked silently for a minute. "Persis, I—there are facts you must know. The estate of Carranca belongs to me, is entailed to Duarte, but my mother has a legal right to live there until her death. That is her *only* right," he said evenly.

"She is Castilian Spanish and accustomed to the deepest formality. One assumed she'd return to her Spanish estate when I married; she chose to remain at Carranca. My wife was semi-invalid, glad of assistance. After her death, Branca agreed to care for Duarte. It seemed a wise solution . . .

"Unfortunately, business kept me away; my father died when I was a schoolboy. His affairs were well managed, but I had everything to learn. In my absence, my mother forgot that her only right is to live at Casa Carranca," Seb finished drily. "She placed the management of her Spanish affairs in Miguel's hands. It developed she also entrusted him with my land."

"Couldn't you have had an estate manager?"

"I did. He left after three months; Miguel bridged the gap until I found a replacement. One man lasted six months; another stayed only six weeks. Miguel is still there."

"Is he not a good manager, then?"

"On the contrary, he's a bit too good," Seb muttered.

Account 24226? While I tried to think how to lead up to it, we rounded a final curve and faced a stark building that seemed planted like a revolutionary barricade across the road.

I forgot Miguel, staring fearfully at the huge bat-wings of the house, with mountains looming in ascending tiers behind, cutting off all sun but a brilliant reflection from the snowcap of a needle-like peak in the distance. Already a trailing thread of mist wreathed the chimneys and was drifting lazily down to obscure clumps of greenery. There was no sign of life, no glimmer of light. It was sheer Edgar Allan Poe, and involuntarily I whispered, "Seb, why are we here?"

"Because there is something that requires my personal attention." He drew the car to a halt before shallow stone steps leading to immense carved wood doors, and finally I caught a faint gleam through narrow side windows. Seb leaned to release my door. "One thing: say nothing of taking Duarte away, *comprendido?*"

I nodded silently, all my fear returned at the ugly devil-mask of his face as he passed the headlights to open my door, help me up the steps. Vaguely, I wondered why there were no outside lights, no servants . . .

Seb produced a key. *The door was barred within.* He stood for a minute, his fingers holding the useless key. Then with a long breath, he stepped back, reached to the heavy iron knocker and battered furiously. At last there was a fumbling beyond, the scrape of a withdrawn bolt, and the door swung open to reveal a trembling white-haired crone (I was still with Poe), whose face was first amazed, then delighted.

"Dom Sebastiao, come in, come in—we did not expect . . ." She bobbed up and down, while Seb strode forward.

"And I do not expect to find this door barred, Josefa."

"*Sim, sim,* but Dona Benedecta commands."

"At Carranca it is I who command. Have the bolt removed!"

I'd never known Seb capable of such rage, but as Josefa agreed, "*Sim, sim,* all will be done," her eyes were turned to me. Instinctively, I tried to soften his anger by a smile—and she abandoned him! She flew forward, seized my hand, and kissed it respectfully. "*Obrigado,* thank you for coming!"

"Thank you for your welcome," I whispered as Seb swung about, his eyes oddly wary as the old woman released my hand.

"Persis, this is Josefa, who was my nurse, but who listens to nothing I say."

"I do, *sim, sim,* all will be done," she assured him,

scuttling over to kiss his hand. "We knew you would find her."

Seb pulled free. "Be quiet!" he said harshly. "Where is Dona Benedecta?"

"In the salon." With a final glance at me, Josefa was gone. Seb frowned absently. "Come," he said finally, turning to a rear hall.

"Now? Couldn't I freshen up first?"

His dark eyes surveyed me critically. "You'll do as you are," he said, and smiled the brilliant smile.

I had no clue to that smile. It seemed a private joke between Sebastiao and himself, not necessarily unkind. I'd often seen it when something I said or did amused him—but twice I'd seen it just before he demolished a braggart with a scalpel sentence. Even as I went beside him, I wondered whether he was with me or against me . . .

Before us, paneled doors with light and soft voices beyond. Seb smiled at me. "Stand up straight, *querida,* and remember you are the wife of dos Martim!" He pushed back the doors and ushered me forward. "Good evening, mother—Branca—how are you, Miguel? It gives me pleasure to present the new mistress of Carranca: Dona Persis dos Martim y Bradbury."

Stand up straight. "How do you do?" I smiled politely, absorbing the scene. A sweet-faced woman with graying hair and hideous space-age spectacles . . . a rotund little man, lolling complacently in what must be the master's chair, judging by the speed with which he was getting out of it . . . and finally, a tiny figure half-lost in a wing chair at the other side of the fireplace.

She wore a sheer black lace mantilla over pure white hair, with a blaze of diamonds at ears and throat, and a formal dinner dress of black chiffon. Beautiful fine bones, olive skin carefully painted, a silver-handled cane beside her, a delicate crystal wine glass held in one arthritic hand—and Seb's cavernous dark eyes regarding me somberly.

It was hate at first sight.

Branca came forward smiling, to kiss me on both cheeks. "My dear sister, how good to welcome you!"

"Indeed yes!" Miguel's oily voice agreed as he took her place. He was two inches shorter than I, with spaniel eyes and a nasty curly mustache. "Aha, you have brought us a prize, Sebastiao!"

"Yes, I rather think I have." Seb poured two glasses of wine, extended one to me. "Chill-medicine, *querida.*"

Dona Benedecta said nothing.

I smiled warmly at my sister-in-law. "So good to meet you, Renée sends her dearest love."

"Here, I think you will find this comfortable, sister." Miguel trotted forward a small armchair with an ingratiating smirk.

Dona Benedecta said nothing.

"Well, mother?" Seb looked down at her compellingly. "I hope you agree with Miguel?"

"*Certamente,* I am lost in admiration." Her voice was a harsh rasp, heavily Spanish, but she smiled thinly, extending a hand. "Dona Persis, you will forgive, it is hard for me to walk . . ." Her tone was odiously meek; I knew she'd have tried this trick even if she could fly like a bird.

So I concentrated on the chair Miguel was presenting, and on the wine in my glass: "Delicious, darling—one of ours?" Then I turned and saw the hand. Instantly I sped to my mother-in-law, not leaning for the conventional two-cheek kiss, but merely patting her hand gently. "No need to apologize, Dona Benedecta! I wonder you even try to walk. Surely a rolling chair would be more comfortable?"

"No doubt, no doubt, but it requires someone to propel and there is still the problem of the stairs," she sighed.

"Oh, the modern paraplegic chairs can be handled alone," I said, bracingly, "and surely there could be a moving stair seat or elevator?" I looked innocently at Seb, to meet a faint gleam, but was it anger or approval?

"A very sensible suggestion," he murmured as an elderly butler came into the room. "Good evening, Roberto. Our rooms are ready?"

"*Sim,* Dom Sebastiao. You pardon? I was in the wine cellar."

Seb nodded brusquely. "We will dine at nine o'clock. Branca, you will show Persis to her room, if you please. Miguel, there is something I wish to discuss with you."

"I am at your service, Sebastiao."

Following Branca, I could hear Seb saying with the most perfect indifference, "You are comfortable, mother? Roberto, attend to the fire, please, and refill Dona Benedecta's glass." Then I saw him striding along a lower hall, with Miguel trotting after him—and through the half-open salon doors, Dona Benedecta sitting abandoned by the fire.

Lying in warm water, soaping away travel dust, I wondered dismally how I'd ever survive the next days. Why had I allowed myself the luxury of bitchery to Dona Benedecta? If Seb couldn't get rid of her, I certainly couldn't, no matter how uncomfortable I made her. Besides, I had a gloomy certainty I was no match for my mother-in-law when it came to poisoned verbal darts.

Branca had shown me to these rooms, leaving me in no doubt of her friendliness, so that was something to look forward to—and tomorrow there would be Duarte. "He spends Tuesday evenings with Mr. Wilson in the village, in order to attend the early Wednesday calisthenics. If Seb had only telephoned, Duarte would have been here to greet him," she shook her head ruefully, "but always that is Sebastiao!"

" 'Come, there is not a moment to lose!' " I grinned at her, and after a startled glance at me, Branca broke into a delightful girlish giggle before turning away to peer carefully at towels, fresh soap, tissues, while I looked at the luggage racks. They held only my cases. "Where are Seb's bags?"

"In his rooms through that door," she sounded faintly bewildered, as though I should have known. "If there's anything you need, Persis, please ring this bell."

The instant she'd gone, I tried the door to Seb's room. It was locked.

So that was something else to consider. For the first time I thought of the separate suites in the Lisbon house. There'd been a door between study and morning room. I'd had the wall between the dressing rooms removed, turned Seb's bedroom into an informal lounge, for evenings we were alone. The locked door at Carranca raised a new concept: was I supposed to be visited, like Marie-Antoinette or Anne of Austria, when it suited my husband?

So far, Seb appeared as willing as Barkis, but I was still a novelty. He'd said if he didn't like what I'd done, he'd have it done over—in which case, I wondered with detachment, which side gets to keep the key?

I was just finishing make-up when the hall door swung open violently and Seb strode in, looking eight feet tall due to the fury in his eyes. "Open that door, if you please."

"Open it yourself, I haven't a key." I watched tremulously while he rattled the knob. "It was like that when Branca left. I supposed the key was on your side."

"You *tried* to open it?"

"Of course. I debated prising with the poker, but I figured you'd open up at bow-tying time," I got up. "Stand still, darling."

"Persis, I—for a moment I thought—" he muttered.

"That I'd locked you out? Not bloody likely—but it goes both ways," I told him evenly. "I don't mind knocking first, but I have a thing about keys: I don't like them. Understand?"

"Ah? If I do not present myself when expected, you will come looking for me?"

"Damn right I will—and you had better be where you're supposed to be, equipped with a cast-iron excuse."

"You are a jealous female! I shall not dare to glance at another woman, or you will claw her eyes out!"

"Hah! I can do better than that; you forget I'm the descendant of a Salem witch," I told him snootily, bending to finish the lipstick. In the mirror, Seb's hand lay on the doorknob, his face sardonic, the lips tight-pressed, frightening.

"No, I have not forgotten that," he said softly. "You are nearly ready, *queridinho?* I will get my jacket."

"Wait!" I said—but once more he was gone before I could ask.

By Dona Benedecta's smile when I entered the salon,
I sensed she wished to avoid a clash, which was a relief.
All the same, dinner was uncomfortable. She sat at Seb's
right hand; Miguel and Branca were to my left and
right. There seemed some sort of overhead fixture, but it
was not in use. We ate by two immense standing
torchères holding tiers of candles—fantastically beautiful but unhelpful for dissecting broiled chicken. The
table was long and narrow with an immense vermeil
centerpiece that obscured Seb, and made the party into
two separate groups. I chatted politely at my end; Dona
Benedecta rasped in a confidential undertone to Seb,
and while I had no particular desire for general conversation, I felt deliberately excluded, shut away.

A tête-à-tête with his mother seemed not to Seb's liking, either. After the third time I'd had to lean sideways.
"I'm sorry, were you speaking to me? I can't see you with
this thing in the way."

"You do not admire it?"

"Infinitely—but you're even prettier, darling."

"Roberto, remove the centerpiece," but after it was
gone, Dona Benedecta stared tight-lipped at her plate,
and Seb was smiling brilliantly. By the wicked sparkle in
his eyes, I knew I'd put my foot in something. Well,
damned if *he* could maneuver me any more than she
could! I turned to Branca, placidly. "Did you see that
article in *Oggi* last month, on Renaissance art?"

"No, no, I missed it," she murmured, shakily

"I thought it good, but I'm no expert. Seb, remind me
to send it to Branca?"

"Yes." In the flickering candlelight, his face was impassive. He raised his wine glass with an infinitesimal

motion toward me before he drained it. Was he pleased or displeased? I couldn't tell—but if he wanted a family fight, let him do it himself.

Half an hour later, he did.

Setting the fragile demitasse cup aside, he said indolently, "I should like the keys for the mistress of Carranca, if you please, mother." He extended one hand without a glance, and picked up his brandy glass, while I sat frozen—but Dona Benedecta was already fumbling in her velvet evening bag.

"*Certamente,* Sebastiao, *uno momento, por favor.*" She drew out a 4-inch steel circle so jammed with keys that I wondered how anyone knew one from another. Seb raised an eyebrow.

"I had not realized so many valuables had been added to Carranca as to require all these new keys, mother. Be good enough to indicate the one for the connecting door of the master's suite."

The gnarled fingers turned and sorted. "Not precisely valuables, Sebastiao," she whined, "but much of the time we are only a household of women, and one feels more secure . . ." She held up a key, extending the ring to Seb, who calmly worked it free and slid it into his pocket. Then he examined the others thoughtfully, and I suddenly realized: it was more than exasperation with his mother's usurpation of power, it was burning anger—almost murderous rage, as though some tiny straw had broken the camel's back.

His fingers stopped at last. "Where is the key to the safe containing the Carranca gems?" Silently, she drew it forth and laid it in his hand. "Better still, we will accompany you while you deliver them to my wife." Oh,

God, he'd really got under her skin! She leaned forward, glaring at him.

"Perhaps you would wish me to take off the necklace I am wearing?" she hissed.

"As well as the earrings and other accompaniments of the Carranca parure," Seb nodded, *"to which you are not entitled."* He stood up lazily, towering over her, forcing her to look up. After a second, she fumbled with a bracelet catch. "Branca?" He stood implacable, sipping brandy while Branca stripped off every jewel, even the diamond-tipped pins securing the mantilla, until Dona Benedecta was only an ugly old woman with a gold wedding ring and a single diamond on her left hand.

He wasn't finished. Holding the diamonds swaying in his fingertips, "I'd forgotten your passion for gems, mother, although surely you persuaded father to equip you handsomely. Where are they?"

"In the safe," she muttered, her eyes fixed on the flashing diamonds.

"So you can have no need of this. I think we must remove temptation at once. Lead the way, if you please."

Silently, she struggled to her feet and hobbled from the salon, with Branca and Miguel beside her. Seb refilled his glass and drained it. "Come, Persis."

"Must I?"

"Yes, you must."

"I don't want the jewels."

"I know. Come."

What would he do if I said, "I can't stand this; get them yourself?" I was his wife, and Sebastiao's wife was mistress of Carranca whether she would or no. I swallowed my nausea and went up the stairs beside him, to find the others waiting outside a door. "You have the keys, Sebastiao," Branca murmured, apologetically.

"Why, so I do." Seb handed them over. "Really, mother, what is this Spanish passion for locking empty rooms? I fear you must conquer it. The mistress of Carranca does not like keys."

Branca opened the door, returned the keys, and we filed in. Seb tugged imperiously at a bell pull and went straight to a panel beside the mantel, which he unlocked to reveal a metal door. Swiftly, he twiddled knobs.

It was a huge safe, literally stuffed with boxes and chamois bags. Seb's eyes widened in genuine amazement, then narrowed sharply. "Well, it seems you've increased your 'pretty pebbles' very handsomely, mother." For a moment, he studied the cache, then with a sort of grim fury, he reached forward and ruthlessly hauled everything pell-mell to the floor. Dona Benedecta moaned involuntarily. Miguel carefully eyed his toes, and Branca sank down beside me so suddenly that I knew her knees were shaking. Impossible to see her expression behind the hideous glasses, but from the fixity of her gaze and her pallor, I felt she'd never seen inside that safe before.

There was a tap at the door. "Come in. Ah, Luisa, turn on all the lights and mend the fire, then wait in the dressing room. We shall be finished shortly."

"*Sim, sim,* Dom Sebastiao." The maid scurried about, casting covert glances at Seb, who seated himself in an immense chair and methodically opened cases, inspected bags, all the while commenting softly.

"The rubies, the pink pearls, the triple strand blues . . . ah, here are your emeralds, mother." He held them up briefly. "A pity they're Oriental cut, but the design is still charming, one of Branca's best. I recall you were unhappy that father could not afford platinum after selling the Oporto house to pay for the emeralds—but now you see it was a blessing in disguise. Platinum is demodé, while gold may be worn any time."

Involuntarily I glanced at Dona Benedecta. Her sharp wizened face was naked in its hunger, staring at the gems; her crippled fingers twitched and curled with unconscious acquisitiveness as Seb replaced the necklace in its box and courteously set it in her lap before returning to his grim inventory.

"Why," he exclaimed in surprise, "here are your diamonds, Branca. What are they doing here?"

"The key to my safe has somehow become lost," she said tonelessly. "Our mother felt my jewelry would be safer placed with hers."

"Surely a new key could be obtained? Miguel, see to it tomorrow."

"Certainly, Sebastiao, certainly. It had merely slipped my mind temporarily during arrangements for spring planting." Miguel hastened to absolve himself. "After all, Branca has no need of jewels these days."

Quite suddenly, I'd had it. "Why not?" I asked ingenuously. "If Dona Benedecta can wear diamonds *en famille*, why should your wife not wear hers, Miguel?"

He looked at me, tight-lipped, but evidently decided discretion was the better part of valor. "A good question," Seb was saying, rapidly separating boxes and bags. "These are yours, *querida irmá*, and these," he tossed a number of boxes and most of the chamois bags back into the safe, "are your property, mother." For an instant, he contemplated the spoils before closing the door and dropping the key into Dona Benedecta's lap. "It appears Miguel has done well with your land, to have realized enough for such superb investments," he observed. "What a pity he achieves so little with Branca's property."

"Scarcely my fault that her land is poor quality," Miguel sneered faintly.

"Ah? We must see how we can contrive to better matters. You will explain to me tomorrow morning, if you please. And now," rapidly he spread out open boxes, "you recognize the hereditary jewels of Carranca, mother?"

She jerked her head. After a moment, she reached forward painfully, closed a box, picked it up and extended it to me. "Dona Persis, I hand you the jewels of the mistress of Carranca." A second box, a third, each with the same formal statement, until I ended with an armload, while Seb slid the bags of unset stones into his pocket. There remained a small pile on a side table.

Seb went through them once more. Snapping shut the last box, he drew up to his full height and murmured gently, *"What* has become of Cristinha's engagement ring?" There was a stricken pause, while Miguel's hands closed over the back of Dona Benedecta's chair, Branca swayed slightly and grasped me for support. Dona Benedecta sat pinpointed beneath Seb's gaze. "Ah, you are wearing it in preference to your own," he discovered with exaggerated surprise. "It is double the carats, of course, but," he held out his hand, "not yours."

For a moment, I thought she meant to lash out at him, but he merely waggled his fingers demandingly, and her eyes fell. Slowly, she worked the huge diamond from her hand, and somehow let it fall to the floor just before it reached his palm. "Miguel," Seb remarked softly, "your cousin's fingers grow uncertain. Will you be kind enough to give her Cristinha's ring once more, *so she may return it to me in person."*

Miguel bent to retrieve the jewel. Seb stood perfectly still, his eyes locked with his mother's. "When will you learn that I shall win in the end, I wonder? Or that the end is close at hand. Hand me Cristinha's ring, mother."

"I am to be blamed for physical disability?" she snarled, but this time the ring dropped into his palm.

He turned it about, reflectively. "Why, as to that, mother, every medical specialist has assured you that your arthritis would improve greatly in a different climate, such as your Spanish estate," he returned, sliding the ring into his pocket. "If you insist upon remaining in an unsuitable locality, I can scarcely be expected to sympathize, *de accordo?*"

"It is my right to live here."

"Yes. However, it is my right to state the rules of management for Casa Carranca. If you wish to live here, you must abide by those rules," he returned, indifferently.

"I'm sure I have given every attention to the wise management of your affairs, Sebastiao." Suddenly, her voice whined ingratiatingly. "You know well that I have spared no effort to preserve Carranca for you, my son. I had flattered myself that the increased revenues, village improvements, were proof of my devotion to your interests."

"Yes," he agreed, "you and Miguel have done well; you will find me justly appreciative." He turned to me, *"Querida,* it has been a long day for you—for all of us, in fact. Branca, take your jewelry and go to bed, dear sister." Seb smiled at her mischievously. "Never mind the lost key, there are few desperadoes at Carranca and Miguel is at hand, after all."

"Luisa?" As the maid popped out of the dressing room. "I believe the day has been longest for Dona Benedecta. Assist her to bed, if you please." Seb held

Cristinha's jewel boxes casually under either arm, nodding politely. "Branca, sleep well, *irmá;* Miguel, ten o'clock in the estate office."

"Sim, sim, good night . . ."

"Persis?"

Robot-like, I got to my feet, clutching the jewel boxes, and made it to the door Seb held open. His face was coldly impassive, "I will be with you shortly, you can find your door alone?"

I was nearly past him, when a recollection of manners swam into my confusion. Automatically, I turned with the heritage of Carranca in my arms. "Good night, Dona Benedecta, *bem sono.*"

For a second her cavernous eyes contemplated my burden, then she smiled at me as brilliantly as ever Sebastiao had smiled. "Thank you, my dear Persis—and to you, also, good sleep," she said tenderly.

And I had the curious impression that she had just decided to kill me.

chapter 9

In my bedroom I dropped the boxes into a chair and turned it to the wall. Slowly I prepared for bed. The door to Seb's room was still locked, the key in his pocket, but I was in no hurry for him to open. I sat brushing my hair absently, trying to think.

Ridiculous—sheer lunacy due to fatigue, to fancy my mother-in-law meant to kill me—but Cristinha had died in this house, and it was the sight of her ring on Dona Benedecta's hand that had enraged Seb. Renée had said, "Stay away from Carranca if you value your life!" But what on earth could Dona Benedecta do to me?

Caterina dos Passos had died here, too—a second tragedy but only an accident, surely? Absurd to envision a crippled old woman crawling around mountains in order to hurl a pebble at a strategic moment—but it is not difficult to create a minor snow slide to cover a sling shot, I thought coldly, and Miguel Revascues is not a crippled old woman.

I shivered involuntarily and scoffed at myself. Shades of Alfred Hitchcock! All the same, I couldn't rid myself of the sense that there was a weird tenuous bond linking everything together, if only I could put my finger on it.

Two deaths of women connected to Sebastiao, plus the curse, and the next cut finger or faulty tractor brakes? No wonder Seb couldn't keep an estate manager; yet why was it so vital for Miguel to be in charge? He could never inherit; even if Duarte died, I knew there were distant male dos Martims somewhere in France.

I threw aside the hairbrush and walked restlessly to the window, pulling aside the heavy draperies to stare at the mountains towering, brooding, in brilliant moonlight. Mid-July, yet a cold chill struck through the glass. I leaned within the folds of the draperies, fascinated by the crystal clarity of the scene. Somehow, Uncle Ted had found his way through that frightening, apparently impenetrable barrier. He'd brought with him hundreds of people, millions of dollars, and never been caught. What would he think of a goddaughter who was a coward?

Not much!

William Bradbury had brought his family to the Massachusetts Bay Colony in 1635; from the deck of that cockle shell called Ye Brindled Cow, the Atlantic waves must surely have looked as tall and threatening as these mountains. What would he think of a descendant who hadn't the guts to speak up?

Not much!

No use to say I must protect others. Caution was still strongly indicated, but the first step was to determine the true basis for my marriage. My ancestors were probably scared to death of Indians and guns at Valley Forge or Appomattox, but they *did* it.

Slowly, I went to settle in a chair by the fire, waiting. I'd just finished a cigarette and thrown the stub into the dwindling fire when there was a soft click and the connecting door swung open. Seb's expression still bore traces of his anger. He stalked in and without preamble, asked, "Where are the jewels?"

"In that chair."

His eyes absorbed the significance of the averted seat, his mouth tightened and he pulled the chair around roughly, so that two boxes slid to the floor. With grim impatience, he scooped them up, and went to a panel beside my fireplace, disclosing another safe. I felt a bit impatient myself, as he transferred everything, and added the chamois bags. "The combination is 2, 4, 6—right, left, right. Can you remember that?"

"Certainly, if I ever need it."

Seb slammed the safe, eyeing me sharply. "You *will* need it," he stated, "tomorrow night when dressing for dinner, Dona Persis. You understand me?"

"Yes. Could you . . ."

"You are going to tell me you will be sickened to wear jewels obtained in this fashion? My conduct is incredible," he interrupted, with deadly softness, "You will obey the command to wear my family jewels, but will have no pleasure in it and are disgusted with me? That is what you wish to say, Dona Persis?"

"Not precisely. Actually, I was only going to ask you to put another log on the fire," I murmured wistfully, "and I should like a glass of sherry and a cigarette." I snuggled more comfortably into the chair without glancing at Seb, aware he was standing motionless, disconcerted. *Dona* Persis? Hah! He wanted a fight? He'd get it! The Bradbury temper had come to my rescue, finally, as it had probably steeled my forebears.

After a long moment, he dealt efficiently with the fire. I kicked off my slippers and wriggled my toes enjoyably, while he silently brought sherry, lit my cigarette. He was still wary. "Is that all?"

"More or less—except that I'm tired of improvisation."

"What do you mean?" Seb was genuinely bewildered.

"The skills you employed for Martim y Antobal did not automatically end with my wedding ring. I'm still able to carry out instructions, further your plans, when I know them. *Why didn't I?*"

He leaned against the mantel shelf, impassively. "Go on."

"You let me sit like a fool, not knowing what to do or say," I remarked analytically, "but you knew from the moment you caught your mother wearing those diamonds, you knew you meant to make a stand on Cristinha's ring. Why didn't you brief me?"

"My family affairs do not concern you."

"The hell they don't! I never even knew there *were* any Carranca jewels," I yelled, springing to my feet. "I arrive for presentation to your mother and sister, on trial: second wife, not only foreign but a former employee. And since I've had no word from your mother, I assume she disapproves, and may refuse to recognize me. A bit nervous-making, *de accordo?*" I was striding back and forth, ignoring him. "Well, so long as you recognize me, I can forget other people—but," I whirled on him, "you don't recognize me as your wife, really, do you, Seb? You not only tell me nothing, you even tried to get me to start your fireworks with that fool centerpiece. I'm not so much disgusted as disillusioned, by your selfish disregard of me." I threw up my chin and caught his gaze squarely. "Why did you marry me, Seb?" I asked clearly. "To be a pawn in some private game, a figurehead sitting speechless at the head of a dinner table while you make the moves?"

"You wish to make the moves for yourself?" he countered softly, his face distorted by fury. "You ask why I married you? I might ask you the same question, *minha mulher*, except that I know the answer." He seized my shoulders, half-shaking me. "Shall I save you the trouble of invention?" he asked harshly. "You married a man old enough to be your father for a title and money, for a magnificent house that will cost a hundred thousand dollars and provides an excellent excuse for trips to Paris unaccompanied by your husband. Oh, yes, I know I was first—but I will not be last, will I, *minha mulher*? How long before another trip to Paris for a new frock or curtains? Bah!" He thrust me away violently. "Well, I have married you, God help me—you have the title, a fat settlement, the money, house, social prestige and discreet lovers, but it is still not enough? What more? A partnership, suited to an American secretary clever enough to marry the boss?"

It was a moment until I could find my voice, but if I'd been angry before, I was now fighting mad. "That's what you think?"

"Did you suppose me so blindly infatuated? You cannot wait even two weeks before putting your plans into operation. The honeymoon is hardly begun, and already you are continuing the career girl, 'sharing' your husband's business," he snorted. "It is scarcely finished before you are 'sharing' the profits to create the finest house in Lisbon—and two weeks later you can wait no longer for the first assignation in Paris. Whom did you meet, I wonder? This Artie, whose miserable ring you cannot bear to discard? *I* have turned you, most respectably, into a woman. I might expect priority for at least a few months, but no," he raved, "you must make haste to use the new freedom at once. Not even possible to use some of the money you spend so freely to telephone the man who gave it to you. Well, *minha mulher*, you are my wife, and my wife you will remain for better or worse, *comprendido?* If you had any American ideas of a future divorce, forget them. You will be Dona dos Martim until I die, there will be no second marriage to a young man of your choice, but," he towered over me, "if you ever hope to live in your palace, you will be very very careful, *minha mulher*, very discreet!"

"I see." Indeed, I did, and it was taking all my self-control to hold my voice steady. "Let me reassure you, Seb: I hadn't planned on divorce, I wish no share in Martim y Antobal. I'm interesed in whatever you like to tell me. That's natural, I think, but if you've no need of a wife to listen intelligently to business talk, by all means change the subject.

"Furthermore," I said hotly, "I *asked* you to say what I should spend on the house and you wouldn't; it's entirely your own fault if it's more than you like. At least, there's a king-size bed in it, and that's all that interests you, isn't it, Seb? Shall we get it quite straight? You want a house to suit your prominence, but you cannot sleep with an interior decorator, so you marry a stupid American girl to display family jewels and share your bed.

"All that troubles you is that perhaps I'm not stupid enough—and you're so right!" I assured him. "Just as you think you know why I married you, you needn't tell me why you married me. I was a nice fresh piece, all for you to add to your possessions. I'm sorry you feel it wasn't worth what you think you paid for it, but buy me a couple of books on sex, *meu marido,* and I'll try to do better, or perhaps," I whirled and swiftly pulled aside the bed covers, "you might prefer to undertake my instruction yourself? Then you'd be certain I'd please . . ."

I shrugged off the robe, stripped nightgown over the head and let it fall. "All right, here it is. Come and get it, such as it is." I was hardly aware I was sobbing hysterically, until I felt Seb's arms about me.

"Shhhh, *querida,* it is not so, we are saying what we do not mean because we are tired, and I have made you angry, shhhh." Seb swung me up in strong arms to the bed, swiftly pulled off his robe and lay beside me . . .

Much later I roused slightly, to think that whether he willed or no, I was quite probably pregnant . . . so at least I'd have something.

Pallid sunshine filtered through the slit-like windows. The connecting door was closed but opened at a touch to reveal a deserted room. On my dressing table lay the key ring. I eyed it, while I combed my hair and, tentatively, let myself remember last night. Seb's furious possessiveness was a major shock, but it explained Shadrach's collar and the dictionary. Could I endure it? "Dos Martim's wife must be his alone," but if Seb didn't know in his heart that I was, how could I stand it? Now I knew the phone calls, the unexpected return from Oporto were only checking up. I'd bet he had verified my presence, my arrival and departure unaccompanied, from each host—because I was only a possession, warned to be discreet, or I'd be stripped of the jewels and dumped in the street.

Make a rhyme, every time, I thought dully, taking my coffee to lean against the window. In daylight, the mountains were even more forbidding. Fancifully, they sym-

bolized my marriage—because I wasn't going to be able
to live this way.

Coldly, I could see myself, turning into a mess of pot-
tage, learning to hate my husband for wanting so little.
Without egotism, I knew there was more within me than
could exist on the superficialities of playing hostess,
Paris-gowned, Martim-jeweled, in a beautiful house. All
my tiny tentative hopes were gone. Seb neither expected
nor wanted a wife to love him. He'd be proud if my
dinners were the best in Lisbon, furious if it ever
emerged that I'd personally prepared anything. He'd be
pleased if Dona dos Martim headed a charity committee
for underprivileged children—and annoyed if I were
out of circulation due to pregnancy.

Not good enough. With my life expectancy, I should
face fifty years of triviality? The mental die was cast:
I'd rather be heartbroken for a while than endure the
slow death of my love. I'd go home, return Seb's settlement and get a Reno divorce. I'd go back to work and
if I never remarried, I'd still have the memory.

Meanwhile, play it straight and to the hilt. A wave of
remembered insult swept over me. He thought I was a
scheming bitch? Give the customer what he wants!

Through the window I could see old Josefa, emerging
behind an outcrop, picking her way skillfully down the
rocky path. She reached a tiny plateau, stopped for
breath, raised her head and saw me. Instinctively, I
smiled and raised my hand, "Hi!"

She curtsied in the middle of the path.

I set the empty cup on the tray, picked up the key ring.
I was mistress of Carranca? Very well, I'd *be* mistress
even for a day—and let's see how much hell I could
raise with a bit of Yankee piss and vinegar! It took no

more than a hand on each knob I passed to discover every door was locked.

The construction of Casa Carranca was simple: two wings, obviously an original house connected with a more modern building by a narrow, pitch-black passageway on the bedroom level. I felt my way forward, emerged on a square hall surrounding a broad staircase leading to a lower hall of exquisite Moorish tiles, and somewhere I heard muffled voices. The near doors were locked, but across the hall a door opened to the schoolroom.

A figure in clerical vestments sat beside a battered oak table, but my eyes were on the boy scrambling to his feet. He was Sebastiao in miniature, even to the wariness in dark eyes, the tilt of the head. We looked at each other carefully, as the padre rose quietly.

It was love at first sight.

"Excuse me," I said courteously, "but do I have the honor to address Dom Duarte Alessandro dos Martim y Francar?"

Duarte grinned wickedly. "You do," he assured me, straight-faced, "but the honor is entirely mine, Dona Persis dos Martim y Bradbury."

After which we broke apart, until the priest chuckled gently. "I am Father Paul, Dona Persis, and most happy to welcome you."

"And I to meet you," I shook hands cordially. "Somehow I feel this should be a half-holiday. Would it be possible for Duarte to show me around, say, in an hour?"

"Of course. He does not go to Mr. Wilson until three."

"It's short notice, but I don't know how long we'll stay," I said earnestly, "so I hope you're free to dine with us tonight, Father?" I knew by the flicker of his eyes, he'd never been invited before. "I'd like Mr. Wilson, too," I went on smoothly. "Would you be kind enough to ask him for me, Father? Seven o'clock, early dinner because of Duarte's bedtime."

I smiled placidly into his pale gray expressionless eyes, and after a moment, he murmured, "Of course. Most thoughtful of you, Dona Persis."

But the corners of his lips twitched faintly.

I found the kitchen. My appearance threw the staff into wild disorder until Josefa emerged to take charge. Two sharp sentences, and everyone was lined up for presentation to the mistress. I moved along graciously, murmuring, *"Obrigado, obrigado,"* and noting the peck order between curtsies and hand kisses: Roberto, Luisa, three maids, a gardener and a terrified tweeny, who fell on her knees to kiss my hand. *"Obrigado,"* I said, hauling her erect, and turning to Roberto. "We will dine at eight o'clock, there will be eight people, serve drinks at seven, if you please."

"Sim, sim."

I extended the key ring. "Open every lock in Casa Carranca, and as you open, remove the key from the ring. I wish to be certain nothing remains locked, *comprendido?"*

"I am in your hands, where shall we go?"

"The gardens, then the stables," Duarte said authoritatively.

"And after that?"

"The village, if you are not too tired." He looked at me earnestly. "I am selfish to keep you, when they have waited so long. Will you have enough strength, do you think, Dona Persis?"

"I expect so; if not, I'll warn you. Lead on, MacDuff!"

He giggled infectiously and dragged me across the lower old hall to a side door. "Tia Branca's garden, but there is never enough sun." I saw spindly rose bushes, uneven beds of zinnias and petunias, and remembered Renée's shiver of distaste. The house was so placed that there was nothing behind it but towering peaks—probably a clever choice of site in the Middle Ages. Carefully, I followed the boy upward until I stood breathlessly on the plateau, with Duarte chattering beside me. "See, these are all our lands—those fields, the length of that road, more behind the trees, all the way to the river, Dona Persis. Is it not magnificent?"

"Yes—but my friends call me Persis," I smiled.

"It is a beautiful name for a witch," he said casually.

I sat down abruptly on the nearest outcrop. "You think I'm a witch?"

He nodded happily. "It was always foretold, Persis. You are the blue-eyed witch from over the water who will lift the curse from Carranca. Father promised to find you, and here you are."

So now I knew it all. I surveyed the panorama before me, another of Sebastiao's possessions and one for which he was prepared to pay for the rest of his life with a loveless marriage? Duarte was talking a mile a minute. "Father may have meant it to be a surprise, but Teresa sent word to Josefa. She says there is even a black cat and a picture of you from long ago, but we would have known at once by your eyes, Persis. They are *most* beautiful," he said admiringly, "like field flowers after a rain."

"Surely you don't believe in witches, Duarte?"

"Not really—but about halfway, Persis—and it can't

hurt to satisfy all the conditions of the curse, don't you
agree?"

"I don't know. Sweetie, sit for a moment, while I
rest?"

He established himself cross-legged beside me. "It's
downhill all the way," he assured me, "and if you're
tired, someone will bring you back." He leaned his head
against my knee in companionable silence, while I
thought rapidly.

To play along, or not? My faith is absolute, but decid-
edly anthropomorphic. Privately, I am certain God has
a sense of humor, as well as total comprehension of mo-
tives: the ultimate psychiatrist, in fact. I am fond of God;
I think His creations are so wonderfully exciting, one
must repay Him by trying to please. But would He like
me to pretend to be a witch in order to get rid of this
silly curse—or would He rather I didn't, because it
would be like worshipping false idols?"

Actually, it depended on what I had to do. "Duarte,
do you know the exact words of the curse?"

"Of course. 'Forever shall ye lose all that ye love
best in life unto the last generation, until the blue-eyed
witch from over the water shall come among you, to
open every door,'" Duarte's childish treble repeated
glibly, "'Yea, even those that are buried and locked
in your hearts.'"

*And already I'd told Roberto to open every door in
Carranca!*

"That's the entire curse?" At his nod, I decided to
play. My innocent order seemed an omen, even if only
inspired by a desire to annoy Dona Benedecta. But of
course, God *knew* that. I got up. "Let's go?"

The village was a cluster of houses and shops along

two streets leading from a tiny cobbled square. Duarte settled me on a grassy shaded bank, "Rest, while I go ahead, please? Only a minute, Persis." His face shone with excitement, the dark eyes danced, and my heart turned over as I watched his eager dash along the street. He was so like Sebastiao . . .

Duarte was banging on the iron triangle beside the horse trough at the center of the square. Up and down the street, doors opened, heads appeared. I couldn't hear what he was shouting, but all the heads vanished. He came running back, catching my hand and dragging me to the nearest house. "Come on, Persis." As we approached a woman emerged, hastily tying on a clean apron, bobbing up and down, smiling—*after which she whisked into the house and quietly closed the door in my face.*

For a split second, I stood disconcerted, until I recalled I was to "open all doors." But I hadn't keys for these. With a gulp, I turned the knob and felt limp with relief when the door swung back to reveal an assortment of women and children. "Senhora Mendoza," Duarte said, and tugged me away as soon as she'd kissed my hand. "Otherwise you won't get to everybody," he told me authoritatively, "and the ones you miss would feel you weren't going to take the curse from them."

"We can't have that," I agreed, pulling myself together. If all I had to do was go from door to door, opening each one, I felt certain God wouldn't mind.

It began to be fun, in a way. There were babies, a delicious odor of fresh bread in the bakery, a festive air, and no doubt of the warm welcome for the mistress of Carranca. I forgot I was meant to be a witch, not that I thought any of these smiling people really believed it, either. It seemed more a pleasant ritual, a charming custom like May baskets or kissing under the mistletoe.

It was still physically tiring, and I was more than happy to crawl into the Carranca car which was mysteriously waiting. Duarte's face was grimy but satisfied. "We did every door! You will not mind to return alone with Jorge, I am already late for Mr. Wilson."

"Run along, then—but be sure you're dressed for dinner at seven."

The dark eyes widened with shock. "*I* am to eat with you?"

I looked at the manly little figure, and the Bradbury temper engulfed me. "You will sit between Father Paul and your aunt," I said evenly. "Take me back to Carranca, Jorge, if you please . . ."

Swaying wearily against the side cushions as the car slowly negotiated the hairpins of the final approach to Casa Carranca, I was raging inwardly. How dare these people confine a well-mannered ten-year-old to nursery quarters, to sleep among servants? Did he eat in the kitchen? I wouldn't be around long enough for any permanent changes, but now I'd done what Seb wanted from me, I decided grimly to amuse myself. If he didn't like it, he could lump it!

Roberto returned the ring, empty but for three keys, "to outside doors, I thought la Dona would wish to retain those. What shall I do with the others?"

"Throw them away, Roberto."

Methodically, I went from room to room, deliberately leaving doors open behind me and taking a good look at the dining room. The electric fixture was ornate, ugly when lit. "Are there candlesticks?" Roberto produced two magnificent silver candelabra. "A centerpiece?" He led me to shelves of china and glass, sadly stated there were no flowers. "Fruit and vegetables, then." I surged to the kitchen, where everyone insisted on kissing my hand before producing the green groceries, but eventually I concocted an arrangement of oranges and lemons, purple eggplant, green peppers, white cauliflower, in a shallow crystal bowl, and laid a handsome cluster of grapes atop.

The entire staff accompanied me in reverent silence while I selected linen, silver, goblets. The table was laid, the centerpiece placed, and the candelabra set slightly askew: one between Sebastiao and his mother, the other a few inches between Father Paul and myself—leaving a clear view from master to mistress. I chuckled naughtily at my *belle-mère's* annoyance.

Roberto looked dubious. "Pardon, Dona Persis, but will the table candles be sufficient?"

The torchères stood against the wall. In daylight they were even more fantastically beautiful, incredibly old. I could fancy early masters of Carranca, dining in regal state overshadowed by their curse. "By all means, let us have them also. Could they be placed nearer the table without difficulty in serving?"

"*Sim, sim.* One stands behind the master, one behind the mistress." Roberto automatically tugged them into place. "La Dona would like the others?"

"Others?"

He opened a paneled side door into a huge empty room, with immense fireplaces at either end, a tiny musician's gallery above. A dozen similar torchères were grouped on the near wall. "The old banquet hall," Roberto said, as I exclaimed delightedly. "How many of the torchères does la Dona wish?"

"One—to stand behind Dom Duarte's chair." Tonight, Dona Benedecta should be forcibly reminded that the heir to Carranca took precedence over her, and if she whined about inadequate light . . . "Roberto, is there another table candelabra? Hold it in readiness, please."

I went wearily upstairs, but while I systematically opened one door after another, too tired to look at the empty guest rooms, something nibbled at the edge of my mind. Before I could identify it, I'd found Miguel's room, untenanted but for the triptych, which sat placidly on a wall bracket over a desk.

Unhesitatingly, I closed the door and searched—not that I expected to find anything. Nor did I, aside from a wardrobe more extensive than Seb's, custom-made even to handmade underpants. That had cost a pretty penny! There was a keyhole in a fireside panel, so he had a safe, and presumably any record of 24226 was there. The desk yielded only a few bills, paid and unpaid, and some terse notes from Pepe, who seemed an old acquaintance keeping a friendly eye on Agueda Grande when Miguel was at Carranca. The most recent message advised that Pepe feared a leak had damaged the library, but he'd removed the valuable books and sent for a plumber.

I went along to the next room, obviously Branca's, but equally deserted. There was a connecting door to Miguel's room, and on impulse, I tried the knob. Behind me, Branca said quietly, "I have the key to that door, Persis; I hope you permit me to keep it?"

"That key is not the privilege of the mistress of Carranca," I said, equally quiet, and turned to smile at her. "I hoped to find you, have you time to spare?"

"Always, my dear sister. Come into my studio." She led the way through another connecting door, and at a glance I knew this was her haven: an atelier. Paints, canvas, easels—but all unnaturally tidy, with a comfortable chaise longue beneath a strong reading light. Tears started to my eyes, looking about me.

Here Seb's sister sat alone, among the ruins of her career, married to a man she'd locked from her bedroom, subservient to a mother who appropriated her jewelry—and Seb had done nothing to prevent it. That huge house in Lisbon? Why hadn't he asked Branca to live there with Duarte, not only well away from a man she detested, but closer to the best ophthalmologists . . .

"I'm so sorry you need eye surgery again," I said experimentally, and was answered by her genuine surprise. "Lunch gossip in Lisbon, I must have misunderstood," I shrugged, "but I'm so glad I was wrong! Can you do any work at all, Branca?"

For answer, she removed a cloth from one easel, revealing a rough portrait of Duarte. "We've been three months on it, there are so many days . . . but we hope to finish for Seb's birthday present," she said evenly. "Sit down, Persis, and tell me of Renée . . ."

Deliberately I put on the blue Paris gown, hunted in the safe and found a parure of sapphires. Hah! Separating the tiny catches, I thought cynically that it might match my eyes better than the zircon but held less meaning. At least, Artie had *given* me the zircon. In the hall beyond my door, I heard muffled motion: Luisa and Branca assisting Dona Benedecta. There was no sight nor sound of Seb. Swinging open the connecting door, I found an empty room, dinner clothes laid ready. Where the hell was he?

Stormily, I swept from my room to the kitchen—where the tweeny promptly dropped a glass at sight of me. Oh, damn this witch business! *"Fique descansado,* sweep it up," I said, while she was tearfully kissing my hand. "Roberto, serve drinks at seven; Josefa, try to hold back dinner until Dom Sebastiao returns."

I went through serving pantry to dining room for a final glance. The fruits and vegetables made a brilliant note of color above white damask, the candelabra and goblets were placed, the torchères stood ready for lighting . . .

"There were details, Persis—the candelabra from the banqueting hall . . ."

"Terribly rugged, but only about fifty miles through the mountains from Agueda Grande to Carranca . . ."

"Father Juan brought a Christmas rose . . ."

Carita's insistence on using precious cargo space for candles . . . the final entry, with no room for details but Uncle Ted would "remember forever, no man could ask for more . . ."

Blindly, I stumbled forward and clung to a chair. That was why there was no record at Agueda Grande.

Uncle Ted had married Elvira Revascues at Carranca —perhaps in this very room . . .

chapter 10

Why had no one thought to search the Carranca parish records? Why hadn't Father Juan revealed the marriage when Dona Benedecta and Branca returned at the end of the war? Or was he, too, dead? Had Dorica been born here, had Elvira died in one of these rooms? Was she buried in the Carranca graveyard? Yet how was it possible no one would know of a new baby, a fresh grave? Who was the doctor, what had become of the parish records?

My head was spinning—and in the entrance hall I could hear Roberto, admitting my dinner guests. I pulled myself together, and swept forward. "Father Paul, a pleasure to see you again—Mr. Wilson, welcome to Carranca."

The Englishman's eyes were shrewd, flicking over me like a snake's tongue and softening to a twinkle. "The pleasure is mine."

In the salon, Dona Benedecta sat, dressed in humble black, with not a jewel in sight.

I recalled the two French courtesans: one wore all

her jewelry to Maxim's—the other entered unadorned,
followed by a maid wearing her loot. "Good evening,
Dona Benedecta. I'm sure I need not present my guests
to you, or to Senhora Revascues." From the corner of
my eye, I could see tight lips, bristling. Dona Benedecta
stared stonily into space, jerked her head brusquely as
the men bowed politely. So she thought herself too good
to dine with a parish priest? "Why, where are your
emeralds, Dona Benedecta?" I asked, brightly. "Don't
tell me you have lost the key to *your* safe, what a pity.
Father Paul, Mr. Wilson—quite too warm for a fire tonight, don't you think?" I settled them at the other end
of the room. "Branca, won't you join us—please . . ."

Mr. Wilson played up nobly, Father Paul's eyes were
thoughtful, and suddenly Dona Benedecta's rasping voice
demanded, "Duarte, what are you doing here?"

"I come to dine with my father."

"Nonsense! Return to the nursery at once, where you
belong."

I stood up. "On the contrary, Dona Benedecta," I said
clearly, "the heir to Carranca belongs beside Dom Sebastiao. Come in, Duarte."

The boy came forward hesitantly, bowed stiffly to his
grandmother. "Good evening, Dona Benedecta. I trust
you are well."

"No, I am not," she hissed, struggling forward in her
chair—and a tall figure strode into the room. "Good
evening, mother . . . if you are unwell, we will gladly
excuse you to dine in your rooms. Father Paul—Edward—good to see you. Duarte, you have grown an
inch!" Seb's face was sardonic, but in a split second he'd
taken over, smiling at Branca, accepting his highball
from Roberto, and facing me. His eyes flickered involuntarily, his body was momentarily still.

"Bem tarde, meu marido," I murmured. "You've spent a happy day?"

"No," he said flatly, as Miguel pattered breathlessly into the salon, "Pardon, forgive the lateness, unavoidable . . ."

"My fault," Seb remarked, his eyes fixed on me. "Persis, *querida,* you find it in your heart to forgive this unworthy mortal."

"Of course, *fique tranquillo,* dinner will be served when you are ready."

He glanced at me sharply, downing half his drink at a gulp. "And you, *minha mulher,* you have passed the time pleasantly?"

"Yes." I felt Duarte's hand stealing into mine. "I have been opening doors." Seb's hand clenched so violently I thought he'd crush his glass. He straightened up like a jack-in-the-box, his face ghost-white. "That *was* what you wanted me to do, wasn't it? Should I have waited for you?" I asked, innocently troubled. "I thought Duarte would do just as well."

"What are you talking about?" Seb asked harshly, and I could feel the child's hand trembling, while Miguel stared at me over his drink and there was utter silence throughout the room. I could see Roberto loitering tactfully to announce dinner, and Father Paul's eyes fixed on me gravely.

"I am talking about the curse of Carranca. I have lifted it from the village," I said indifferently, "but I suppose there may be outlying farms, requiring transportation. Do you care to come with me tomorrow, or shall I do them alone?" My eyes flicked about the room, from Branca's hideous spectacles to Edward Wilson's intent expression, to Miguel's narrowed eyes. Only Dona Benedecta's reaction was unseen, alone in her fireside chair—but I'd caught the convulsive grip of hand on cane.

I rose smoothly, pulling Duarte with me, and smiled, "Surely you all knew that I am the blue-eyed witch from over the water? I wasn't married for my *beaux yeux*, but my blue *yeux*, padre."

"You believe yourself to be a witch, Dona Persis?"

"No, indeed! But apparently others do. Shall we go in to dinner?"

For a moment, there was only silence while Seb's eyes blazed at me. Then he said contemptuously, "An old wives' tale! Let me hear no more of it, if you please."

Under cover of table conversation, "Father Paul, there is a matter on which I should like to consult you. . . . If you could spare a few minutes before Duarte's lessons tomorrow?"

"With pleasure, Dona Persis . . ."

Duarte was dismissed to bed, bowing very correctly over each hand and giving mine a tight squeeze. "Is that all I get?" I asked, disappointed. "I thought all Latins were born knowing how to kiss a woman."

He giggled shyly and kissed my cheek. "Good night, Persis."

"*Bem sono, meu coraçao!*" I hugged him heartily, and looked up to meet Dona Benedecta's inscrutable eyes.

Now I was certain she meant to kill me.

The evening ended finally, with polite thanks from the guests, and Dona Benedecta hobbling away with Branca and Miguel. I was turning toward the stairs when Seb commanded, icily, "Stay, if you please, *minha mulher*." As he was between me and the door, gracious compliance was obviously indicated. I turned back and sank into a chair; he closed the salon doors and strode forward. "Now—what is this nonsense of opening doors? What have you been doing?"

"Just that: opening doors. I understood that was all I had to do. It seemed harmless, so I did it."

"Por deus, where had you this—this fairy tale?"

"From everyone but the person who should have told me first," I said evenly. "If we're going to talk about it— and I assure you we are, *meu marido!*—I should like a drink and a cigarette. You'd better have a drink yourself, you're going to need it." Seb opened his mouth furiously, he never had a chance. "How DARE you involve me in these shenanigans without warning?" I demanded, passionately. "Whether or not you believe in your curse, everybody else does—including your son! You started the whole thing, dammit, you called me a blue-eyed witch the first night I wore this dress, and Teresa heard you."

Seb closed his mouth and stood rigid, remembering. *"Por deus,* so I did," he muttered, "but it was only a joke."

"She didn't think so—and because I didn't know what it was all about, I only made things worse, by showing her the miniature of Old Persis. She may be a 'simple peasant mentality,' " I snorted, "but she still knows I'm American and America is over the water. I even have a black cat. What more is wanted?"

"You're right—I need a drink," he said, splashing brandy into his glass. "I never thought, I swear it—it was simply that evening." He downed the brandy at a gulp, and pressed his hand to his forehead, despairingly. "When I saw you, I said the first thing that came to mind, but I never meant . . . go on, please."

"Teresa sent word to Josefa, who alerted everybody.

Duarte finally told me the wording of the curse. I'd already told Roberto to take the keys and open everything." I looked at him squarely. "I'm no giant intellect," I remarked; "perhaps you can suggest an acceptable alternative to going from house to house and ritualistically opening each front door?"

"That is what you did?"

I nodded. "From the general air of *en fête* when I left, I fear Miguel will lose a day's work due to major hangovers tomorrow."

"He's likely to lose more than that," Seb muttered, his lips slowly curving into ironic amusement. "As God is my witness, Persis, I never planned it this way—but if you have convinced the tenants the curse is lifted, Miguel is out of a job." Suddenly, he threw back his head, roaring with laughter. "Oh, Persis, *minha mulher,* by God you *are* a witch! In a few hours you accomplish what I couldn't do in fifteen years!" he gasped, helplessly, turning to refill his glass.

"I'd be interested to know what you did plan," I remarked, dispassionately, "but if you're meaning to discharge Miguel, I can tell you he won't feel any pinch."

Seb stopped laughing. "What d'you mean?"

"I mean that along with all the other Machiavelli tactics in your family, Miguel Revascues has a Zurich account, #24226." I drained my glass and set it aside. "If you'll forgive me? It's been a tiring day, I should like to go to bed."

"Not until this is explained." Seb's hands clenched cruelly on my shoulders.

"Why? Does Macy's tell Gimbel's?"

"Ah, the business woman again! Very well, *minha mulher,*" he said deliberately, "I will give you half— half, do you hear?—of Martim y Antobal in return for facts that will enable me to get rid of Miguel Revascues forever. As you say in America: is it a deal?"

"No—and remove your hands at once, please." When he'd stepped back slowly, "I have a counter-proposal. I'll tell you anything I know," I said in a low voice, "for the right to have Duarte visit me during school vacations in America. I'll return your marriage settlement, never think I won't! I'll protect your pride with a quiet Nevada divorce and no fireworks unless you cause them. Is that a deal?"

"You—wish to leave me?"

"It seems strongly indicated. Well?"

"Agreed," he said, finally. "Begin, if you please."

"Miguel has a sideline, sales of rare art objects. His salesroom is the apartment below ours, where I was inspecting rotted draperies one day at Teresa's request. On a table was a medieval triptych, a ruby glass and gold chalice. Miguel sold the chalice to a Mr. Kupperman for five thousand dollars, payable to Zurich 24226 'as usual.' "

Seb drew a sharp breath. "When?"

"While you were in Oporto, but not the first time I'd heard sounds downstairs. I don't know which Zurich bank, or I'd have tried to get the current balance."

"They wouldn't have given it to you," he said absently, pacing back and forth, concentrating with growing satisfaction.

"So there you have it. May I go to bed now?"

"When you've told me why you think Miguel sold a fake," Seb agreed softly. I sat silent, while he reflected, "Because that is what you think. You've known this for weeks; you tell me only when you are privately certain my sister Branca, whom you know I love, is not involved. Well?"

"Feminine intuition," I shrugged, but I was choosing my words carefully now. "I'm no expert, but I'm positive the triptych was genuine. Kupperman offered fifty thousand dollars for it, Miguel refused—but if it wasn't for sale, why was it there at all, Seb? Why was he so worried he might have been overheard? Why does he only use the place when you are away, and leave it so tidy that Teresa swears to me no one has been there in years?"

Seb nodded. "Something else makes you positive of trickery."

"Yes," I told him, reckless through fatigue, "but for once, *meu marido,* you will damn well take it on faith that it does not indicate one of these numerous lovers you're so certain I possess." I threw open the salon doors to face Roberto, patiently waiting to clear and lock up. I looked back at Seb's thunderous *NO* expression. "You will excuse me," I stated politely. "It's been a tiring day."

I was nearly asleep when the connecting door opened. In the final flickering embers of the fire, Sebastiao walked toward me. "So you mean to leave me, *minha mulher?*" he said conversationally. "I must make the most of what little time remains to me."

And he did . . .

chapter 11

"How can I help you, Dona Persis?"

"By searching the parish records from mid-December of 1938 to October of 1939."

"What do you want me to find?" Father Paul asked quietly.

"Reference to a marriage ceremony performed at Carranca on December 23rd—a girl born at Carranca in August—a death sometime in September."

"What names shall I look for?"

I sat silent for a moment. "Father Paul, am I right that if no crime is involved, you can grant the seal of the confessional to anything told you in confidence?"

"Yes."

"Then—I have reason to believe Señora Revascues was smuggled across the border during 1938 and was living at Carranca, that her daughter Elvira joined her mother about December 23 or 24—and that on the night she arrived, she was privately but legally married to a Theodore Anderson," I said steadily, "that the ceremony was late at night, took place in one of the rooms at Carranca and was witnessed by her mother, performed by Father Juan.

"That is what I want to find, Father Paul. It's more important than the birth or death records," I said earnestly. "For various reasons it might have been kept secret, but somewhere there has to be a record."

"I will search, of course, but at that time the Carranca parish priest was Father Leon," he murmured, frowning. "He was elderly; in fact he died only a year after I was sent to assist him. You are sure of the priest's name, Dona Persis?"

A deathbed mumble might have mistaken Juan for Leon. "No," I admitted. "I'm only sure the marriage took place, resulting in a child, and that Elvira Revascues died of pneumonia shortly thereafter. Her mother took the baby to the Martim town house in Lisbon, where she died a few years later."

Father Paul nodded. "Why does this concern you so deeply?" He smiled at my hesitancy. "You are promised my silence, and I may say Father Leon was devoted to the family. He might well have concealed records if he were convinced of a need for secrecy."

"It was needed, all right; it still is. If you find the records, we must invent a way to discover them by accident."

"Why?"

"Because they will legitimize Miguel Revascues's niece, thus forcing him to transfer half his inheritance."

"He won't like that," Father Paul agreed drily. "How did you happen to suspect this, Dona Persis?"

"Theodore Anderson was my father's half brother and my godfather—and his daughter has inherited his hands." I met the priest's keen eyes squarely. "And

Theodore Anderson was better known in these parts as Rico Andes," I finished evenly. "That is what must be concealed."

Very slowly Father Paul's lips curved into a broad smile, while he studied me. "You are his goddaughter!" he said reminiscently. "I never met him, my parish was near Almeido then—but once, in the middle of the night, someone came. A woman was dying, Rico Andes required a priest for her." He smiled again. "I felt proud to be asked, but," he stood up briskly, "you are right that this must be hidden. Have no fear, Dona Persis. I promised silence; it is double silence for his sake. Although," he remarked, judicially, "I'm not sure the mere mention of your relationship might not have raised the curse as quickly as opening doors."

I laughed helplessly. "I didn't know what else to do," I confided. "Seb was furious, but it was his fault, really —and if I'd refused, don't you think the village would have gone into mourning? But when I got to the parish house, I wouldn't open the front door, I went around to the kitchen," I said earnestly, "so that shows, doesn't it? I wasn't being sacrilegious; I pretended I was only visiting everyone. Please don't disapprove."

"I don't," he grinned. "You have lifted the curse, and it was a masterly touch to open my back door. He would be proud of you." Father Paul's face went serious. Very deliberately he made the sign of the cross, laid his hand fleetingly on my forehead. *"Pax vobiscum,"* he murmured, turning to the door, just as it opened to admit Seb.

He stopped short at sight of the priest. "I felt I should explain the witch business," I said, smoothly. "Thank you for your understanding, Father."

"Thank you for your courtesy, Dona Persis," he murmured, equally smooth. "Good morning, Dom Sebastiao."

"Good morning," Seb said automatically. "You do not disapprove of this affair?"

Father Paul shook his head placidly, "If you could see the smiling faces in the village," he remarked, "you would be happy that such a simple action could produce peace and reassurance. Dona Persis, Dom Sebastiao, I bid you good day; Duarte's lessons are waiting."

When the door had closed, Seb eyed me sardonically. "Clever, *minha mulher!*"

"Yes, I thought so," I agreed, refilling my coffee cup calmly. "What's on your mind?"

Seb's lips tightened. "Dress and pack as quickly as possible, if you please. We are returning to Lisbon at once." He strode forward. "Where is the key to the safe?"

"On the dressing table."

Once more all the boxes and bags were hauled out, tossed in an untidy heap on the bed. "If you have not space, I can make room in my cases. Can you be ready in an hour?"

"I can be ready in thirty minutes, provided you get the hell out of my way . . ."

I had to stuff most of the bags into the side pocket of my handbag, but fortunately it was one of the huge models. It was disgustingly bloated, but I managed without having to open that connecting door. In twenty-five minutes, my cases were closed, the door swinging open, Roberto was carting Seb's bags down the stairs. "Come back for mine, please."

I went to the narrow passage for the old wing, and heard Seb's voice. "Where are you going?"

"Where I'd expected to meet you: saying goodbye to your son," I told him. "But of course I should have known better. How infinitely stupid of me to think you'd spare a thought for him. He's only another of your possessions, isn't he?"

"Nonsense, the boy is at his lessons, Roberto will tell him later," Sebastiao said impatiently. "Come, if you please."

I glanced at my watch. "I still have five minutes. You may wait in the car, you son of a bitch—and I use the expression in its literal sense," I said softly. "All that matters is that you have a son. The hell with whether he sleeps and eats with servants; never mind that nobody hugs or kisses him, and any servant can tell him—when they happen to remember—that his father has arrived or left. Who d'you think you are, God?"

Seb recoiled, white-faced, braced against the handrail, and I glanced at my watch again. "I've wasted a minute. I want it back," I said contemptuously. "You aren't worth a minute compared to your son. Wait in the car, or wherever you wish—preferably in a gutter, if there is one."

"I'm sorry to interrupt, Father, but Dom Sebastiao wishes to leave for Lisbon at once. Goodbye for the moment, Duarte."

"So soon? You were hardly here," Duarte's lips quivered.

"I know; I'm sad, too, darling." I held out my arms, and he burrowed against my shoulder unhappily.

"It will not be forever," Seb's voice remarked. "You will see Persis again, she has made this a condition for the future—but in the meantime, we must start at once. Goodbye, Father. I have no fears for Duarte so long as he is in your hands. *Até logo, meu filho."*

After a final hug and kiss, I let Duarte go and stood up, while Seb looked at his heir. *"Até á vista, pai,"* the boy said, uncertainly, holding out his hand.

"You are ten, it is time for correct forms between father and son," Seb smiled the brilliant smile, brushing aside the boy's hand and bending for the two-cheek embrace. *"Até á vista . . ."*

In silence we descended the stairs of the old wing. In silence, we disposed ourselves in the Ghia, and in silence drove a hundred and fifty miles to Lisbon. Once, on the Coimbra by-pass, Seb began, "Persis . . ."

"D'you mind? There's nothing more to say."

In Lisbon, my bags went up to the apartment. "I regret, I must be away on business for a few days. May I hope to find you here on my return, or is your departure immediate?"

I looked at Seb's stony face and longed to hit him! "Oh, I shall be here," I assured him sweetly. "There are still a few odds and ends to tidy up. I trust you've no objection?"

He nodded. "Necessary to send advance notice for the homecoming celebrations? But so long as you remain in Lisbon, where else would you stay but in your husband's home? *Até logo,* until we meet again." He was almost out to the car before I found my voice.

"Hey!" I leaned over the rail. "What do I do with these damn jewels?"

"What would you like to do with them?"

"Throw them in the nearest trash can," I said hotly.

"Reprisal for a zircon? You have my permission to do whatever pleases you," Seb retorted, and then vanished.

In the street, I could hear the Ghia revved, tearing away.

I went into the apartment and shut the door. I opened my bags and neatly transferred the Carranca gems to the bedroom wastebasket, after which I flung myself across the bed and howled, rolling back and forth, wiping away tears on the edge of the coverlet and occasionally blowing my nose on a handful of Kleenex until I was drained, limp, exhausted to the point of amnesia. I kicked off my pumps, rolled over and was instantly asleep.

I took the jewels out of the wastebasket next morning, of course. "Teresa, is there a wall safe?" It was in the study, and fortunately it was open. I thrust everything inside, closed and twisted the dials. Let Seb open it.

Now, when it no longer mattered, the house was taking shape. Daily I kept myself too busy to think, unpacking china, glass, linen, supervising the hanging of draperies, mirrors, pictures. Finally, it remained only to stock pantry and refrigerator, and we were in business. Minor details: a chandelier must be raised two inches, a carpet was not the shade I'd ordered and it would be two weeks before the manufacturer could rectify, Baccarat hadn't sent the champagne glasses with the rest of the order—things like that. Walking through the rooms after the workmen had gone forever, I was amazed to find so little wrong, modestly elated at my success with a job so completely unfamiliar.

I sat in the shaded living room, smoking a cigarette wearily, and thinking it was sad to have spent so much money for nothing. The nursery would still be vacant; the bedroom and study I'd furnished so carefully for Duarte's use as teenager and then young man-about-town would never be used. With detachment, I wondered whether Seb would sleep in the bedroom meant for us, or pay to have his old bedroom restored.

At least there was nothing yellow nor spindly-legged anywhere!

Would Seb tell the next wife, *"Por deus,* I do not like blue and green, or Danish modern!" I stubbed out my cigarette in one of the ashtrays I'd so gleefully found in the Flea Market, and took a final look at the home I'd created but would never inhabit. Now, this house was no longer static. It was agog with expectancy, waiting for vases of flowers, lighted candles, cheerful voices and laughter. I stood up and said, "I'm so terribly sorry, I did my best and you're really perfectly beautiful, but you have to understand I couldn't be contented only with you. I do hope you get someone to love you . . ."

Teresa was unhappy. Upon firm probing, she confessed she'd not thought we would return so soon, had dared to hope for a few days in which to attend the wedding of a cousin near Santarém.

"But why should you not go?"

"Who will look after la Dona?"

"La Dona will look after herself," I assured her drily, "and the sooner she gets used to it again, the better."

Shadrach took one sniff of Teresa's traveling valise and howled in despair. "I had promised he would go to the country with me," she said, troubled. "Would la Dona allow him to come?"

"You'll have more fun alone, and he's spoiled rotten as it is."

I lay on the terrace in suspended animation, but for my mind which was working overtime. First, stay in Salem until I'd pulled myself together—mummy and daddy would be sad, Bradburys don't divorce, but they

would never reproach me, never imply *I told you so.*
Arrange to return the furniture shipped from New York
as soon as it reached Lisbon . . . have to find a new job,
new apartment. Daddy's lawyer could handle returning
Seb's marriage settlement, and Uncle Ted's nest egg
would tide me over financially. Dorica? Whether or not
Father Paul found anything, we could be friends as well
in New York as Lisbon.

On the first day of Teresa's holiday I struggled with
a preparatory letter home, outlining what I suspected
about Dorica and trying to phrase the marital situation
with dignity. On impulse, I took out the triptych and set
it on the desk. It did seem to make things easier and more
peaceful. When I'd finished daddy, I tackled a definitive
farewell to Seb. I had no idea where he was nor when
he'd return, but I'd promised to be here—and I knew
with dismal honesty that the instant I saw him I wouldn't
be able to think clearly. Whatever I wanted to say must
be prepared in advance, calmly and dispassionately, because there was not going to be any fight, any bitterness.
I was determined about that.

After three hours, I'd managed to write, "Dear Seb,
You've accused me of wanting a house, a title, lots of
money and a share in your business. There was only one
thing I ever wanted: you. I expect I'm just a sentimental
American with a teenage mentality, but I don't know
how to be married without love . . ."

At that point the telephone rang. I picked it up, half
suffocated with hope, and a male voice said, "Dona
Persis, this is Edward Wilson at Carranca."

"Oh, hello. How are you?" I was faint with disappointment.

"I'm well, but Duarte isn't." His neat English voice
was troubled. "Perhaps it's presumptuous of me to

bother you, but Seb's office said he was out of town."

"Duarte? What's wrong?"

"Another bout of tonsillitis; he's been needing a ton-sillectomy for several years, but Dona Benedecta says Seb will not approve." Mr. Wilson's voice became more animated. "I took the liberty of phoning, in hopes of per-suading Seb, because the longer the operation is deferred, the more difficult."

"Yes, I know. Does the doctor say he can do it at once?"

"By tomorrow or next day, although it can wait a week or so."

"Where's the nearest hospital for Carranca? Will you make arrangements, Mr. Wilson? I'll be there as quickly as I can make it," I said decisively. "Thank you for call-ing." I could hear muffled voices, then Mr. Wilson said, "Father Paul asks me to tell you he's found what you want."

I closed my eyes and clung to the phone. When I could control my voice, I said, "I'm still here, tell Father Paul I'll see him as soon as we've got Duarte settled."

I tossed overnight things into a bag, telephoned Sen-hor da Velma, "Tell Dom Sebastiao his son is ill—not serious, but I have gone to Casa Carranca." Shadrach was snoozing on the terrace; I had him into the cat car-rier before he realized, although he had plenty to say as soon as he woke up! He was still grumbling morosely as I hurled the Porsche around the hairpin curves leading to Casa Carranca.

In a hundred and fifty miles I'd had time to think, to feel damn certain Dona Benedecta had never mentioned the need for a simple childhood operation to Seb. Why hadn't Branca told him? Supposedly she was only at Car-ranca to look after Duarte. I recalled the spidery adult handwriting on the envelopes for Duarte's weekly letter, and knew that no letter came in or out of Carranca without Dona Benedecta's censorship. Yet if Edward Wilson could phone, why not Branca, even if she had to borrow the phone to do so?

It was many miles before I could answer that, but finally I thought Branca was physically unable to fight because of her eyes, mentally numbed by the combination of mother and husband ganging up on her, and—in the light of my own experience—perhaps she thought her brother didn't care to know anything of his son aside from a weekly letter, an occasional report from the tutors.

There was a minor legal problem: was I, merely a stepmother, legally able to authorize surgery? I didn't give a damn; I meant to have Seb's son out of that foul prison, no matter what! If the local doctor baulked, I'd bring Duarte back to Lisbon and Doutor Silva, until Seb returned . . . and if he really disapproved, I'd give him a tongue-lashing he'd never forget.

I pulled the Porsche to a stop before the main entrance, found the keys Roberto had given me for the outside doors, found one that obviously turned the lock—and encountered bolts. Seb had ordered them removed; within a week they'd been replaced. Very quietly, I withdrew the key, made my way to the door in the old wing and, as I'd expected, encountered more bolts.

So Dona Benedecta was throwing her weight around the moment Seb's back was turned? I went back to the car and released Shadrach, who instantly secreted himself chastely among the bushes, and was so grateful to have been spared the humiliation of An Accident that he sprang into my arms when he came back. Tickling his neck absently, I went around to the kitchen, where there were lights and cheerful badinage. The door swung open beneath my hand; I walked in, holding Shadrach in my arms and producing instant silence.

The tweeny dropped whatever she was holding and burst into tears. *"Fique descansado,* sweep it up," I said automatically. "Roberto?"

"Sim, sim, Dona Persis, I am here."

"Are you?" I pinched Shadrach enough to produce a faint hiss of protest. "You were told to remove the bars from the doors. Why are they replaced?"

"Dona Benedecta commands," he whispered after a moment.

"Whom do you serve, Roberto, the Spanish tarantula, or the blue-eyed witch from over the water who lifted the curse from Carranca?" I asked softly. "Shall I put it back?"

There was a unanimous groan. "No!"

"Remove the bars at once. I suppose all the doors you opened for me have been reclosed?"

"Sim," he agreed. "Dona Benedecta has duplicate keys, but," Roberto looked into space, "as it happens, I had not yet had time to throw away la Dona's original keys."

"Ah? Then you will be able to reopen, without disturbing Dona Benedecta," I said smoothly. "Prepare my room, and Dom Sebastiao's; Dom Duarte will sleep there. He will have his dinner served on a tray at seven o'clock, and I will have mine in the dining room at eight. Roberto, take one of the torchères to Dom Sebastiao's room for use while Dom Duarte eats. Where is Dona Benedecta?"

"Luisa dresses her for dinner, she descends shortly."

"Then I will inform her of my arrival, you will say nothing. It will be a—surprise." Shadrach had scented food and was struggling in my arms. "Josefa?"

"*Sim, sim,* Dona Persis."

"This is Shadrach, who loves Teresa dearly and will love you equally well so long as you feed him." I deposited the cat in her respectful arms, and went to the dining room. The table was laid for two places, with the vermeil centerpiece and a torchère behind the master's chair. Hah! "Roberto, remove the centerpiece, and replace the candelabra; set the torchère behind my chair and remove the setting for the master. Lay Senhora Branca's place at my right hand." I turned quickly enough to catch an unguarded gleam of satisfaction in the butler's eyes, before he went impassive again. "*Sim, sim.*"

"Dona Benedecta's dinner will be served in her suite. I will be with Dom Duarte; when the rooms are ready, let me know."

Roberto straightened up. "*Obrigado,* Dona Persis," he said with quiet meaning. "I may send word to Father Paul and Senhor Wilson?"

"Yes, please." The significance of two table settings suddenly registered. "Senhor Revascues?"

"Is not expected."

Duarte's joy at sight of me set the seal on my fury. We were both close to tears while he clung to me, whispering hoarsely. "Oh, it is so good you have come!"

"Of course I came, as soon as I heard you were sick. But you will soon be well again, and meanwhile you'll sleep in your father's room, so I can keep an eye on you. What d'you think of that?"

It was almost too much happiness—but there was still a small problem. The connecting door had been relocked, and this one key was in Seb's possession. "Break open that door, use a hatchet if needed," I said to Roberto, "and never mind the noise."

Duarte was comfortably propped against the huge pillows of Seb's bed. His tousled dark hair looked like a single blueberry in a bowl of cream, and Josefa sidled in with Shadrach in her arms. "You permit?"

"I was about to send for you," I smiled. "I place Dom Duarte in your charge, Josefa. Keep the room warm, give the medicine when it is time, and watch over him. Duarte, here is Shadrach to help amuse you." The cat pulled free of Josefa's grasp and leapt to the bed, sniffing delicately, walking forward on velvet paws, while Duarte reached for him eagerly, "Come, Shadrach, come here . . ." Shadrach inspected the child for a moment, then he said "pprrrrrMMMEW" and kissed Duarte's nose.

"I never had a cat before," Duarte said rapturously, as Shadrach settled down, blinking affectionately. "Dona Benedecta doesn't like them."

Well, that figured. I left him stroking Shadrach, who was purring like a steam engine, and went to clean up. By the time I'd washed hands and freshened make-up, Roberto had the connecting door open. He'd used a kitchen spatula because, he informed me, he couldn't find a strip of celluloid such as used in the cinema—which only confirms the far-reaching effects of Hollywood.

"*Obrigado,* Roberto." I found Duarte asleep, his hand still laid on Shadrach's head. Gently I picked up my cat. "You're going to be a witch's familiar, and you better do a good job or no more chicken wings, you hear?" His yellow eyes regarded me unwinkingly for a second. Then he kissed my nose, so I knew he knew I meant it. "I'll come back when Dom Duarte has his dinner," I told

Josefa. In the hall, infinitesimal sounds told me Roberto was already opening doors; clever old man, to have kept those keys! He knew the old lady!

I went downstairs to reconnoiter. In the main salon, resplendent in her jewels, ensconced in the comfortable chair by the small fire and graciously sipping sherry, sat Dona Benedecta—entirely at ease while her sick grandson was, for all she knew to the contrary, lying alone in an unheated nursery, out of earshot. Branca was in attendance, proffering cocktail goodies, although her face was strained.

Once more the Bradbury temper swept over me. I forgot everything but the filthy defiance of Seb's orders; I forgot I wasn't going to be his wife, had no reason to back him up. Instinctively, I was springing to the rescue, knowing exactly what I meant to do with the old hellcat in automatic wifely defense of a husband.

Quietly, I pushed open the door and walked into the salon, holding Shadrach in my arms. "Good evening, Branca—Dona Benedecta, I see you have found the key to your safe. I felt sure you would."

The effect was all I could wish! Seb's mother turned white as a ghost and fell back in her chair with a gasp, while Branca sprang up hesitantly. "Persis! My dear sister, I didn't know . . . that is, we did not expect you."

"So I see." I went forward and the old woman found her voice. "Take that beast out of here at once, I do not tolerate animals in the house," she rasped gutturally, glaring at me.

"How unfortunate—for you," I said indolently, continuing across the room and extending my hand imperiously. "Give me the duplicate keys, and then you may return to your room. Branca, you and I will dine at eight, I hope that's not too late for you but I promised to sit with Duarte while he has his supper." I'd got to within a few feet of Dona Benedecta, who was staring glassy-eyed at the cat. Good heavens, the woman was an ailurophobe! Shadrach knew it, of course, and earned some extra chicken wings by a deep menacing growl, bless him! "The keys," I repeated, politely.

Shrinking into her chair, her eyes still on the cat, Dona Benedecta produced another steel circle from her evening bag. "Thank you. If you have any more, you may as well throw them away. Tomorrow a locksmith will alter every lock at Casa Carranca. There will be two keys for each: one set for the master, the other for the mistress." I seated myself in the master's chair, holding Shadrach on my lap and stroking him gently with one hand, twiddling the key ring in the other. "I think, along with the rolling chair, we should get you a hearing aid," I said thoughtfully.

She pulled herself forward in her chair and spat at me, "What do you mean by that? I advise you not to try any of your cheap American wisecracks here, Dona Persis!"

"That was no wisecrack," I said, surprised. "The use of this key ring proves you must be growing deaf. Only a week past, Dom Sebastiao told you in this very room that keys would no longer be used at Casa Carranca. Or is it the forgetfulness of old age?" I murmured sympathetically. "Either way, the master's orders must be obeyed."

"How dare you speak to me in this manner? Who and what are you? An American nobody who cleverly entrapped my son," she sneered. "Pah! You will treat me with the respect I deserve, *Miss Nothing!*"

"I will indeed," I agreed sweetly, "and as you deserve no respect, you will receive none. Your only legal right is to live at Casa Carranca for the rest of your life—so you will live that life in your own room. Branca darling, will you ring for Luisa? If I get up, Shadrach might leap . . ."

Branca rose, twisting her hands together. "Persis, please—you don't know what you're doing," she whispered, agonized.

"On the contrary, I know exactly what I'm doing, sweetie," I said softly. "I am the mistress of Carranca. The mistress of Carranca does not choose to find a pensioner seated in her living room, appropriating her chair, issuing orders and decrees."

"Pensioner?" Dona Benedecta spluttered furiously.

"What else are you? Living rent-free in a comfortable room with bath for the rest of your life," I laughed lightly. "All old ladies should have it so good! But," I narrowed my eyes, unsmiling, "henceforth that is all you will have, and," I smiled again, "never think you'll change any order I give.

"I expect that curse was extremely useful to you in some way," I remarked thoughtfully. "You were so quick to try to close all the doors the instant I left— but you see it didn't work. The blue-eyed witch from over the water is back again when least expected, and this time she has brought her cat. Once more all doors are open, and this time there will be no retreat, Dona Benedecta. The orders *I* give will be obeyed to the letter —or the curse of Carranca may return."

"You are mad, there is no curse," she raged, "and if there were, d'you think you could alter it? Pah! Get out of my sight, you American bitch!"

"Not I, but you," I said as Luisa entered the room, with Roberto hovering behind her. I stood up, still holding Shadrach; we both looked at the maid. "Luisa, are you aware that I am the mistress of Carranca?" She nodded uncertainly. "Are you also aware that I have lifted the curse from Carranca?"

"Sim, sim," she nodded vigorously, smiling.

"You would not wish it to return?"

"No!"

"Then you and the rest of the staff will be very careful not to displease me, but carry out my orders to the letter?" She nodded again. "Listen well: Dona Benedecta will no longer leave her room, Luisa. You understand? That is my order!"

"Sim, sim, Dona Persis," she whispered, wide-eyed.

"Dona Benedecta's meals will be served in her room, she will not descend to the salon at any time, whether or not Dom Sebastiao is at Carranca. She will no longer be served in the dining room at any time. *That is my order."*

"Sim . . ."

"Aside from requests that concern her personal comfort and health, the staff will ignore any order she attempts to give. Now, please assist Dona Benedecta to her room, and," I turned to Roberto, "to make quite certain she does not forget again, you will take the bolts you have removed from the front door and place them on the outside of Dona Benedecta's room, Roberto, where they are to be used whenever she is left alone."

The butler's face was white with shock, while he nodded. Branca looked ready to faint, and Dona Benedecta's face was alarmingly flushed. She leaned forward, screaming at me in Spanish, which I don't understand too fluently, but there was no doubt she was calling me every name in the book.

"That's enough," I said stonily. "Old ladies shouldn't be over-excited, it's bad for the blood pressure. Roberto, be kind enough to assist Luisa."

The servants went forward uneasily, and Dona Benedecta squatted into the chair like a toad, gripping the
arms and clenching her teeth. "I do not go," she hissed.
"Am I to be turned out of my own salon by a parvenue
who wishes to queen it with her husband's possessions?
Oh, no, you do not get rid of me so easily. It is my right
to live here, and here I will stay! We shall see what Dom
Sebastiao says of this outrage! Ah, you will learn respect
for your betters, my girl."

"Your mind wanders again, Dona Benedecta," I told
her, sympathetically. "This is not your salon, nor your
house or servants—and I expect Seb will be tickled pink
I've found such a simple solution to this problem of your
'right.' Now, will you go to your room, or shall I have
you forcibly removed?" For a long moment she glared
at me, her lips trembling with venom, until I said, very
softly, "We both know I will."

Then I went to the far end of the room, where I looked
from the window to the last tiny rays of sun piercing
through the mountain passes, down which Uncle Ted
had brought Elvira and the candles to light their wedding. Tomorrow I would decide with Father Paul how
best to declare Dorica's legitimacy. If Duarte were well
enough, I'd get him to hospital. After that, my chores
would be done and I could leave. "Branca, faça favor,
bring me a glass of sherry? My arms are full of Shadrach."

Silently, she brought the glass, her fingers shaking so
that the wine cascaded down the stem. Beyond her, Dona
Benedecta was disappearing into the hall. "I'm sorry,
Branca."

"Do not apologize, Persis," she said, surprisingly. "It
has been needed for a very long time, but as you see,"
she held out her trembling hand, "I have not the cour-

age." She smiled faintly, finishing her own sherry and setting aside the glass. "Would Shadrach allow me to hold him?"

It was after four a.m. that I woke to feline caterwauls: Shadrach wanted out. Drowsily I climbed into robe and slippers, shivering in the pre-dawn mountain chill, and picked up the flashlight I've learned always to carry in unfamiliar houses. I'd left the cat with Duarte. Quietly I opened the connecting door, but there was no sign of Shadrach. The child was sound asleep, Josefa snoozing in the armchair by the half-dead fire, but she opened her eyes vaguely as the torchlight swept across her. "Shhh, it's all right, I'm only looking for the cat."

"He was here, Dona . . ."

"He's gotten out somehow, I can hear him. I'll have to find him, you go back to sleep."

"Sim, sim," she mumbled, struggling out of the chair. "First, I mend the fire."

I went out to the hall and down the main stairs. I could still hear the cat yowling, but apparently receding. I supposed he was searching for any possible door, but he'd had no time to learn the house. "Shadrach, here I am, m'nou, m'nou, m'nou, come this way," I called softly, going toward the old wing, flicking the torch about to get his attention, but there was only a despairing *miaoul* and no black shadow bounding toward me. He'd probably get into one of the rooms, couldn't find his way out.

I came into the lower old entrance hall, pausing at the edge of a huge old Oriental rug laid at the bottom of the stairs to call again, "Shadrach? Where are you, baby?"

There was a lugubrious howl, somewhere ahead, followed by a furious hissing and spitting: he'd got involved with something that was giving fight. A rat, perhaps? Hastily, I went across the hall, the torch focused on the farther wall—and exactly midway of the staircase, I stepped into *nothing*.

I had time to realize there'd never been a rug in this spot before, time to throw up my arms to shield my face and instinctively pull my body into a protective ball. Then I was falling down—down—down into icy blackness, without breath enough even to scream. I could feel sharp rocky projections abrading my arms as I fell into a painful heap.

And at the top of the shaft above me, a circular section of the upper floor slid across and quietly settled into place with deadly finality.

chapter 12

Between shock and the bleeding scratches on my hands and face, I lay stunned for heaven knows how long. I may even have dozed briefly, which is nature's automatic restorative—but finally I was capable of ratiocination again.

Slowly, my mind began to work, picking up speed as it went, so that I knew, first, that I was alive. Next, that I might be bruised, but was probably otherwise undamaged, since I felt no specific pain. I shifted position gingerly, explored my various joints and apparently they were still operating normally, though stiff from the graveyard chill of the oubliette.

Because that was obviously what it was: a medieval trap in which to lose inconvenient people, strategically placed exactly where anyone crossing the hall or going up or down the stairs couldn't avoid it.

My hand still held the electric torch; apparently I'd pressed the off switch as I fell, for when I tried the switch, I had light! I seemed to be at the bottom of a circular pit, dirt-floored, about five feet in diameter, with rough-dressed stone walls and a forbidding iron closure at the top. There were spiky projections here and there on the wall that had caused the abrasions as I fell.

A wonder I hadn't broken my neck, I thought—and caught my breath in horror. *Cristinha broke her neck; she was found at the bottom of those stairs above my head.*

I pulled the padded skirts of bathrobe tightly about me and mentally went into orbit. My hand found cigarettes and matches in a pocket; I lit a match experimentally, and the flame flickered! There was a current of air, seeping through the stones behind me, so it would be safe to smoke while I thought.

Cristinha, first: what could such an apparently stupid dimwit have learned that made it necessary to kill her— because she'd been murdered as surely as they'd tried to murder me. *The reason I'd survived was my height.* Cristinha had been a foot shorter, her stride correspondingly less. Where I had stepped into the middle of the open oubliette, been able to break the fall by a half-grasp on the edge, compress my body and plummet straight down, she would have stumbled, fallen forward and neatly broken her neck on the opposite side of the opening.

I wondered when and how Miguel meant to get me out of here. It could only be he, acting on Dona Benedecta's behalf. Tchk, I'd slipped badly there! I should have told Roberto to wrench out any telephone in her rooms. Where was I meant to be found? Couldn't use the nursery bit again; Dona Persis had no reason to be in the old wing. He'd lured Cristinha by a crying baby, lured me in search of my cat, but remembering Shadrach's furious snarling, I had a hunch Miguel would bear some nasty wounds . . .

Shadrach—they'd kill him! Perhaps they'd feel so sure I was dead, they wouldn't wait.

I scrambled awkwardly to my feet, frantic to get out, to save Shadrach. Under minute examination by flashlight, I saw that the projecting rock segments formed a sort of staircase, no more than toeholds irregularly spaced—but what if I arched my body across the shaft? It was possible to work up, bracing on the projections opposite from those at my feet. Slowly, I inched up, until I was at the iron cover— and there was a projecting rock slab that must have been meant for a top step, because it was wide and sturdy enough to kneel on while I tried to raise the lid.

One side shivered; the other was fixed. Dona Benedecta and her keys, I thought bitterly—but this one was never on the ring. I felt cautiously around the rough iron and encountered a metal bar. Automatically I tested it, pulling this way and that, and with a metallic screech, it moved across the shaft so unexpectedly that I was nearly overbalanced and fell to the bottom again.

In the light of the electric torch, I saw it was a rusty inner bar, now holding the iron cover immovable. After a moment, I grasped the significance of this, and with a grim chuckle, I began slowly working my way down. I acquired some new scraped fingers and a nasty scratch on one leg, but eventually I made it. I allowed myself another cigarette, and squandered three matches to identify the other exit; there had to be one, or why that upper inner bar?

It was a huge block of stone. I felt around and around, and finally hit a sort of granite knob. It was above the door, and anyone shorter than I would have needed a ladder to reach it. I had to use both hands and all my force to turn the thing. Evidently it hadn't been used in years, but at last there was a click and the stone opened a few inches.

My heart was suddenly pounding with dread. All the "horrid sights" depicted in medieval romances came flooding to mind, until I was convinced a rat-infested crypt lay beyond. All the same, if I were to escape Miguel, I was going to have to open that door. Holding my breath and listening carefully, I could hear no sound. The air was fairly fresh. It still took every bit of my courage to push and step forward shakily, flashing the torch inside, only to discover a perfectly innocent storeroom.

I sat on the nearest crate and laughed until I was half-sobbing with relief. Here, the exit door was quite obvious. I thought vaguely that I must be under the kitchen; the door would lead either to the wine or root cellars, and if Roberto had followed instructions, it would not be locked.

I lit a cigarette and looked about curiously. The chamber was piled high with cases arranged neatly along the walls. Several long sausage-shaped rolls must be rugs, but the paper was crumbling with age. Everything was relatively dust-free, a minimum of cobwebs in corners, the floor even seemed swept—but as I poked about, the more puzzled I became. Why would anyone store such lovely things? Holland covers hid six magnificent Empire side chairs, an old sheet covered a regal mahogany chest. The drawers contained bibelots: a dozen exquisite miniatures of men and women in what I dimly recognized as Spanish clothes of the seventeenth and eighteenth centuries.

Why were they put away? I picked them up one by one, enthralled by the artistry, and smiling at the simpering coquetry of a pretty miss holding a fan.

On her hand was a diamond-shaped gold ring.

Carefully, I replaced the miniatures and looked about with a wildly pounding heart—*knowing that here was everything Elvira had patiently smuggled to safety.* In other drawers I found table silver tarnished beyond identification, damask cloths, linen sheets crumbling at a touch, a small portrait of a handsome man with a top hat cocked rakishly and an intricately arranged neckcloth. Even as I focused the flashlight I knew the signature would be Goya. It was.

Miguel Revascues had called his sister a thief, yet here were his family valuables. Was this the source of supply for his business? Flashing the torch around, I knew Miguel hadn't the faintest idea—otherwise, there'd be no unopened boxes and crates. He'd have gone through everything, to see what was where.

But someone knew, someone had kept the storeroom clean for twenty-six years. Roberto?

I made for the farther door, and for a panicky moment I thought it was barred, but eventually I pushed it back and stepped breathlessly into the root cellar. No wonder the door was heavy: a triple row of wooden slat bins filled with potatoes, onions, cabbages, was fixed to the door, cunningly matched to adjoining wall bins and shelves! Exhaustedly, I pressed it into place and turned —to face Josefa, one hand pressed to her mouth.

"You have opened even the door that was buried," she whispered.

"Yes." Now I had nearly all of it. Josefa was 9. "You kept it beautifully clean, Josefa. Thank you." I looked up at her commandingly. "Why did you never say that Rico Andes was married here, Josefa?"

She shook her head, despairingly. "He forbade it, Dona Persis. The night he had to leave—because they had found him, *comprendido?*—he said, 'I leave everything to you, Josefa, until I send word,' but then—it all happened so quickly—the baby, the death, the leaving—and Teresa sends word he is dead. Later, the grandmother also." Her eyes filled with tears. "I did not know what to do."

"You did exactly right," I told her soothingly. "I am Rico's niece, Josefa. He would be proud of you!"

"His niece?" she breathed, aghast. "Then that is why . . . oh, come away quickly, before they find you." She turned and scuttled up the steps, reconnoitering at the kitchen door and beckoning to me urgently. I trotted after her, infected by her alarm, but . . .

"The cat—I must find him!"

"Shhh, m'nou, m'nou," she hissed, snapping her fingers softly—and Shadrach bounded through from the pantry. "He found his way back to me while they cleaned your room, Dona."

"Cleaned?" Automatically, Shadrach in my arms, I followed Josefa through the back door, the mist, away from Casa Carranca.

"Sim, they will say la Dona left before dawn, who knows why or where she went."

So I wasn't meant to be found at all? I shivered uncontrollably. "Who are 'they'?"

"Senhor Revascues and his friend . . . they come in the helicopter, as always. Be careful here—the stones are slippery."

"Where are you taking me?"

"To Father Paul."

"Dom Duarte?"

"He will be safe, they do not fear a child, Dona."

Somewhere in the distance was a racing motor: Miguel? He'd already found the barred oubliette, was com-

ing to search for me? Between terror and icy dampness
striking through my bedroom slippers, I was weeping
childishly, stumbling blindly through the dawn fog,
clinging to Josefa's hand. I could hear the car coming
closer and closer, yet seeming to be approaching from
the wrong direction. Josefa ignored the sound, leading
me steadily forward, until I realized we'd circled the village and the parish house was only across the cobbled
street—but now the motor was nearly upon us . . . and
for a brief instant of panic, I wondered if she'd deliberately led me into another trap?

I slid away, clutching Shadrach and wondering wildly
whether I could make a break for the parish house before the car reached us. Josefa was peasant-strong; in a
second she'd thrust me beneath a tree between two village houses, was silently holding me behind her . . . but
through the leafy branches I'd glimpsed a black Ghia
racing hell for leather toward the village square, along
the Coimbra Road.

I threw off Josefa's hands, dropped Shadrach, and
plunged toward the cobbled street, waving my arms
and screaming hysterically, "Seb, SEB!"

I remembered his startled face, the screech of brakes,
his tall figure pelting toward me—*and there was still the
sound of a racing motor.*

Tearing recklessly around the final curve from Casa
Carranca was the Porsche, and for a long moment I
stood spotlighted in the distance beam of the headlights.
Then Seb had literally thrown me onto the cobbles, his
body shielding mine and rolling me over and over, until
we were behind the car—and I was aware of another
man, crouched beside the Ghia, of gun shots, and a
hideous screech as the Porsche was swung desperately
toward the side street.

Between the wheels of the Ghia, I could see the off-wheel of the Porsche catch the stone coping of the horse trough. With sickening speed, the car turned turtle and burst into flames—and for the first time in my life, I fainted.

It was a most peculiar sensation. I felt floaty, inert, dreamily euphoric—aware, yet resisting awareness—unwilling to open my eyes, even to move. Mmmmm, I was comfortable; for tuppence I'd have gone to sleep, except for Seb's voice saying wildly, "Oh, God, they've killed her! Persis, *queridinho,* beloved, don't leave me, open your eyes, sweetheart, speak to me! Where is the doctor? For God's sake, save her!"

My face was wet; sleepily I knew Seb was crying, rocking me back and forth in his arms. Skillful fingers held my wrist, moved gently over my bones. An authoritative voice said, "She has only fainted. Take her away before she revives."

"Yes, please, my toes are so cold," I murmured, and with a groan of relief, Seb gathered me close, kissing me frantically, and struggling up to his feet. Vaguely, over his shoulder, I glimpsed lurid leaping flames, sensed confused motion and shouts. Full memory returned in a tide of horror: the shots, the car, Miguel burning to death . . . I screamed involuntarily, writhing in Seb's arms, and fainted again.

The instant my eyelashes fluttered, Shadrach crooned, "Prrrm'you!" and kissed my nose. For a moment, I lay shivering; what a horrible dream. Then I turned my head slightly, to meet Duarte's bright eyes, and I knew it was no dream, after all. He was cuddled under a blanket in his father's arms, and Seb was asleep, his face gaunt with weariness, his long body uncomfortably propped between a huge chair and ottoman. Duarte smiled relievedly, pursed his lips, "Shhhh!" Shadrach had no compunctions. So long as mummy was safe after this anxious night, the hell with anyone else. He sat up and talked to me, loudly and at length, interspersing his mews with kisses.

Seb opened his eyes and stared at me. His fingers moved an inch to grasp mine. Duarte sat motionless, and Shadrach padded over me, working his way onto the boy's lap. My three men looked at me in silence. I got the message. "We seem to be a family."

Seb's hand tightened. "I found your letter," he said conversationally. "It appears I've been rather stupid, haven't I?"

"I can't imagine how you ever got to be head of an international corporation," I agreed. "Even Shadrach can say 'I love you.' "

"Duarte," Seb said, instructively, "you are about to receive your first lesson in the art of making love. Listen carefully, while I tell Persis that her voice delights my ears; the way she walks, moves her hands, raises her chin, are music in motion. A man could drown in the beauty of her eyes. The expressions of her face are as varied as sun and shadow. The clarity of her mind, the honesty of her soul, are more than any man should expect. Her loyalty is absolute, even to the risk of her own life."

I could feel myself disintegrating inside, but Duarte only nodded judicially. "That is well expressed, father. Go on."

"When we are apart, I do not live; I merely exist until I return to her. Love and happiness were only words before I met her," Seb said deeply, "so that I nearly lost her through my incredulity. What do you think of such a stupid father, Duarte?"

"I expect it'll be all right. You found out in time, and Persis loves you enough to forgive you, if you don't do it again." Duarte pushed away the blanket, stood up, holding Shadrach. "I think it is time for my medicine," he said carefully. "Excuse me?"

"With pleasure," Seb told him softly. *"Querida . . ."* he swung over to the bed, pulling me up into his arms. "I am a foolish old man, insanely infatuated by a beautiful young girl—but I can be forgiven? You will let me try again?"

"Do you love *me*—not just a body, or blue eyes, or a society hostess?" I asked earnestly. Seb nodded. "Do you *know* I love you? I've never had a lover, never expect to have one." I could see Father Paul standing quietly at the door. "Theodore Anderson was my Uncle Ted," I told Seb clearly. "He was my father's half-brother, and Dorica Andreas is his daughter, because he married Elvira Revascues downstairs in the dining room."

"The marriage is documented in Father Leon's private diary," Father Paul came forward, speaking to me. "He meant to enter it in the parish records when the danger was past; there are even blank spaces, but he died too soon."

"Danger?" asked Seb.

"Theodore Anderson was Rico Andes. Elvira was one of his refugee smugglers," I said, *"And all the Revascues family valuables are in a storeroom behind the root cellar.* Josefa took care of them." I grinned drily at Father Paul's startled face. "What price I'm not a witch, after all? I've got blue eyes, I've opened every door— even those that were buried!"

"I can believe Our Heavenly Father might send a

kindly witch for His own purposes," Father Paul's lips twitched, "but to convince me, you must finish the prophecy. 'Yea, even those that are buried and locked in your hearts.' "

"If my heart is acceptable, it was the first door she opened." Seb pulled my hand against his cheek.

"Yes, I thought so." Father Paul chuckled. "Now that you know, there will be a lifetime in which to discuss it—but meanwhile, M. Rouland has some questions."

"Oh, Lord, I'd forgotten him. You feel able, *querida?* It is the agent of Interpol." Father Paul was beckoning forward a politely smiling man with keen hazel eyes.

"Interpol? In my bathrobe?"

M. Rouland chuckled softly. "You are more beautiful in *déshabillé* than any man should expect," he assured me, "and *grande tenue* will only drive other women to despair, Dona Persis."

"Heins, quel blague!"

"Mais non, je dis seulement ce qu'on voit à l'instant, s'il n'est aveugle, Madame."

I laughed helplessly at the bland twinkle in his eye. "I warn you my husband is of a jealous temperament."

"That is no doubt why he routed me out of bed at midnight, to drive here like a—a cosmonaut," Rouland agreed. "I'm sorry to disturb you, but it appears you are the key, Dona Persis. The sooner you turn it for me, the sooner I shall go away."

"What do you want to know?"

"Everything, I'm afraid: how you knew of the Swiss account, why you suspected art forgery, and exactly what happened tonight. Please, Dom Sebastiao," as Seb protested violently, "your wife is an American woman; she can do it."

"It'd be easier with coffee and a cigarette . . . and if I knew how Interpol got into the act."

"There were rumors, someone selling art objects that were occasionally fakes," Rouland said. "It was cleverly done. Reliability was established first, with genuine pieces; then the sale was so arranged that the buyer dared not complain for fear of tax fraud."

"Yes, I thought so."

"Why?" he asked sharply.

"The triptych. If I had the mate for it, I'd have had the chalice if there were one."

"Tell me, Dona Persis."

I told. Everything. Interpol is surely to be trusted, after all? But there was still thin ice. Why had I returned the diaries to America? "It was advised," I said evasively, "because not everyone is dead." The Interpol man pursed his lips, but let it go. Seb wasn't fooled; he knew it could only be Luis. His eyes widened, his expression was clearly, *"Por Deus,* the plucky devil!"— but he said nothing.

Why hadn't I told my husband at once? More thin ice. "I thought perhaps my sister-in-law might be involved. The instant we met, I knew she wasn't, but there were other problems."

Rouland let that one pass, too. "What happened tonight?"

"I arrived unexpectedly, to find my husband's orders had been defied by his mother. I took appropriate action; she sent for Miguel, who opened the oubliette and lured me into it by pinching the cat until he yowled."

"But father sealed it, years ago," Seb muttered hoarsely. "It was only a stairway to the wine cellar, but the steps were crumbling . . ."

"Yes, they're all gone but a top step," I agreed, steadily. "That was one key that wasn't on your mother's steel ring—but because I'm a foot taller than Cristinha, I didn't break my neck." Seb closed his eyes with a groan. "I'm sorry," I whispered after a moment, "but that has to be it, though I don't know why."

"I knew," he said painfully. "I didn't know how, but I always suspected it was contrived. Cristinha was ill at ease in society. Lisbon was anxious for her, so she meant to live here. She said it would be healthier for Duarte—but she wasn't stupid, only timid and shy."

"Twice as dangerous. With not too much on her mind, she'd have tumbled to anything out of the ordinary at once," I nodded. "I wonder how they managed Caterina . . ."

"Miguel was with the skiers," Seb winced, aghast.

"Where was Pepe, I don't know his last name."

"Lariscos," Rouland said quietly. "How did you know of him?"

"Some innocent notes in Miguel's desk, plus feminine intuition—and there were two men in the Porsche. I expect Pepe was driving; Miguel would have known how to avoid the coping of the horse trough." There was a long silence.

"What more do you surmise, Dona Persis?"

I thought about it. "Dona Benedecta was the top banana," I said suddenly. "I don't know how it began nor why, but she had the sucker list of wealthy people, to whom she introduced her cousin, and I expect the numbered account was really hers." Rouland's pen jerked involuntarily. "I'm sorry, Seb, but I think she had something on Miguel. He was a weakling; almost anything would have been enough to force him into shady business, if it meant money for him, too. You should see his handmade underpants!" I snorted.

"Anything else?" Rouland's tone was odd.

"Well, I expect it began by fudging the estate accounts, but the money didn't come in fast enough," I said uneasily, "and then Pepe turned up. I guess he was a real crook, and Miguel's helicopter was made to order. Dona Benedecta took her cut off the top for using Carranca as a way station. First, it was just a fencing operation. Probably most of her unset stones were prised out of stolen jewelry. Later they expanded to art objects."

The Interpol man was staring at me, pen suspended over the notebook. "Yes," he swallowed hard. "You're a bit frightening, Dona Persis. Go on, please."

"That's all, really—except that Dona Benedecta decided to kill me when Seb took away the Carranca jewels."

Rouland's lips twitched. "Did she tell you so?"

"No, but I knew."

He looked at me curiously. "Then why did you deliberately return last night?"

"Duarte was sick," I said, surprised, "and of course I didn't know how she meant to do it. Miguel wasn't here, and I thought I'd have time to get Duarte away, but I forgot she'd have a phone in her room. Stupid of me," I sighed. "I should have told Roberto to rip it out before he put the bolts on the outside of her door."

"What?" the men chorused, incredulously. Rouland got it first. "That was part of the 'appropriate action'?"

I nodded. "Her only right is to live here," I said simply. "That doesn't include freedom of movement. So I said if she wanted to stay, she'd live in her room, and I told the servants if they obeyed her orders, I'd put the curse back. I'm sorry, Seb, but I couldn't stand it!

"She'd locked everything up all over again," I told him shakily, "and Duarte was sick in that horrid nursery at the other end of the house, with not even a fire to keep him warm—and she was sitting in the salon, decked in diamonds, ready to eat her dinner from the master's chair. I lost my temper. She's been using that curse for years to keep everyone scared to death so they'd stay away. I figured I'd make use of it, too, even if you're furious with me."

Seb shook his head, wincing. "I should have realized," he said in a low voice. "I knew, as soon as Interpol came to me. When I was a small boy, she used to give me bags of rubies or pearls to play with—she called them 'her pretty pebbles,' and no matter how many she had, she always wanted more. She was the ugly duckling after the famous 'Five Antobal beauties,' but by good luck she married best. Father's death was a very real tragedy: no more carte blanche at Chanel or Cartier, no more grand balls or *fêtes champêtres* at Cliveden or Château Rothschild. She had more than enough to live comfortably. There'd have been more if she hadn't spent so freely." Seb sighed. "Father was rich, he denied her nothing, treated her like a doll. He married her out of a convent, never expected her to know the value of money.

"I don't know if he loved her, but she was a good wife by his standards. She gave him children, she did not refuse even after I was born. I had a younger brother who died of diphtheria when he was five. Hard to believe now," he said evenly, "but she was a witty, amusing woman. Father enjoyed her company, he was proud of her social success. It contributed to his business ventures. The only time he ever raised his voice was when she bought the emeralds, and it caught him when credit was stretched to the limit for business expansion. After that she was more careful, but he died before he'd replaced the capital loss, and she couldn't accept the loss of her social image.

"I was only a schoolboy. The trustees said there was plenty of money—and there was, but it was mine, no longer at my mother's disposal. The trustees made that legally clear to her the first time she had a bill she couldn't pay; they said nothing to me. They knew she couldn't afford her way of life; I didn't. All I knew was that nothing was changed financially for me, and after the mourning year, mother was buying clothes in Paris again.

"Now I realize: she was only forty-one, she hoped for a second wealthy husband. She had a good chance. An older man wants more than surface," he said, "and age is relative. I am now her age then, but I do not feel old, except in competition with younger men."

"A waste of time when one has no competitors!"

His hand closed warmly on mine. "Mother used her capital to stay in the swim, and the war ruined her. If she'd been in Portugal, she might either have got to the States and continued trying, or retired to Carranca, saving her money for the end of the war. Instead, she was trapped in Turkey with Branca, where there was no society and she was forced to use capital for nothing.

"Until I dug it out these past weeks, I'd no reason to know her finances." He twisted restlessly in his chair. "Oh, I was at fault, I should have inquired, but we were never close. After I went to school, I scarcely saw her for years. Then I was taking charge of my own affairs, and later, business was all I had. My wife did

her duty, but when Duarte was born, she made it clear
. . ." Seb shrugged. "I let her do as she chose, I didn't
care."

Rouland tactfully lit a cigarette, while I wondered
whether I'd ever in a lifetime be able to make up so
many lost years to my husband. Poor boy, now I could
understand his apparently callous treatment of Duarte;
he'd had even less. Seb drew a deep breath. "I thought
my mother lived here from pride. Anything was better
than to be the ugly Antobal widow. Her sisters would
have lost no opportunity of reminding her, 'How are
the mighty fallen!' Actually, she had no choice.

"At the end of the war she had nothing but Agueda
Verde. She could live here at my expense, try to replace capital from the land, or sell jewels, invest and
live quietly in a better climate. Branca thinks she considered selling, but the market was low, and she was
six years older. She knew she'd lost her chance for a
good second marriage. The society she'd known had
vanished; she was too old for the Jet Set. So she kept
the gems and absorbed herself in acquiring more. In a
way, Branca had lost her chance for life, too. I don't
know how she was persuaded, nor whose idea it was,"
he said in a low voice, "but she married Miguel—who
split her dowry with my mother, and got the management of both Agueda Verde and Agueda Grande."

"First to last, every idea was your mother's," I said.
"I'm sorry, Seb, but if you had an inventory, you'd
find a number of small treasures mysteriously missing.
The original goodies had to come from somewhere,
darling. If you'd ever noticed a gap, she'd have said it
had been sent to Coimbra for repair."

"The Medici silver bowl," he muttered, shaking his
head.

"Yes, I expect they stole you blind. The original goodies had to come from somewhere, but judging by Kupperman the buyers are giving them good homes." I sighed. "I wonder who had the goblet he wanted."

"It is in the pantry of the Lisbon apartment, and he will still pay three thousand for it," Rouland said.

"You've talked to him?"

"*Naturellement.* He was most cooperative, since he's not liable to a charge of tax fraud," Rouland observed drily. "He admits he might have been caught very shortly. You were uncannily right, Dona Persis! Revascues found himself penniless aside from an empty house and unproductive land. He applied to his cousin Dona Benedecta, thinking she was rich. She graciously allowed him to manage her property with his own; he was a good manager, but the money did not arrive fast enough even when Dona Branca's dowry plumped the pockets." Rouland eyed me expressionlessly. "Dona Benedecta finally learned that Miguel was a bigamist."

"You mean that horrid little greaseball managed to get two women to marry him?" I protested incredulously.

"Not all women have your discrimination," he grinned. "*En effet,* this Pepe was Miguel's brother-in-law. It's possible Miguel honestly thought himself a widower. Dona Branca states he told her he'd been married, the girl was killed in Teruel. She thinks he believed this, and I'm inclined to agree, because she remembers when Lariscos first came to Carranca.

"He asked for Miguel, who greeted him warmly—but later she chanced to see them emerging from the estate office. Pepe was jovial, Miguel was obviously shocked, white-faced. Shortly occurred the accident, the eye surgery—most expensive for a man being blackmailed.

About a year later, Lariscos again came to Carranca. Miguel was away, Dona Benedecta was descending the stairs. Your sister is certain it was a first meeting, but Lariscos was suave. A few courteous words, and Dona Benedecta offered a glass of sherry before he left.

"That is all Dona Branca knows. It was time for eye drops and a half hour rest. When she descended, the man was gone—but I think we may assume Dona Benedecta learned of the bigamy and reached a meeting of minds with Pepe. Again, you were right, Dona Persis. The man was a petty thief. Dona Benedecta turned him into a master criminal. He was good material," Rouland conceded, "fairly intelligent and educated.

"She admits she provided introductions, forced Miguel to cooperate. She knew some of the locked rooms might, occasionally, contain items not belonging to Carranca, but she saw and heard nothing. So long as she got the jewels, she was deaf, dumb and blind . . . and with her backing, Pepe finally became the focal point for every major robbery anywhere in Europe. The swag was gotten to Agueda Grande, transferred to Carranca by helicopter, placed in a locked room, and disposed of at leisure. Miguel made an extra commission on whatever he sold personally. Checks for 24226 marked 'less 10 off' were automatically split on deposit. There is," Rouland consulted his notebook impersonally, "something over seventy-five thousand in Miguel's account, and just under nine hundred thousand in Dona Benedecta's—which poses a major question: what is to be done with the money?"

By Seb's agonized face I knew it was time to end it. "Interpol will place both accounts in escrow, pending settlement," I said. "Work up a list of Miguel's clients as best you can, to check against major robberies. Dona Benedécta surrenders all unset gems; some of the stones will be identifiable. Will Interpol front for us, if we do the clerical work?" Rouland nodded. "Then we buy back the frauds and offer to purchase legitimate items, no questions asked by Uncle Sam. There'll still be some money. You won't find everyone, and some people will rather pay tax to retain what they bought. It'll take time to straighten out. Some of the jewel owners have had the insurance, and won't want unset stones returned." I shrugged. "I think you've enough to go on with, M. Rouland?"

He eyed me sharply, glanced at Seb and stood up. "Dona Persis, *je vous remercies mille fois!*" He kissed my hand gracefully, bowed himself away to the door, shaking hands heartily with Seb. "No, no, I can find my way, do not disturb yourself, Dom Sebastiao. I shall put matters in hand, while you put them out of your mind, and shortly I shall be in touch with you. *Au revoir, à bientôt . . .*"

Seb closed the door and leaned against it wearily.

"Who loves me?" I asked, seductively.

"Everyone, *queridinho!*"

"Oh, sad stuff," I pouted. "Who wants a crowd?"

"You can be content with me alone?"

"Of course. Why settle for Mount Monadnock when one may have Everest?"

"Now what, dearest?"

Seb was silent for a moment. "Duarte will go to school, we will visit your family, we will return to live in Lisbon. The house is very beautiful. If only I'd called da Velma first . . ." He closed his eyes, "But when the apartment was deserted and I read your letter, I think I was a little out of my mind, Persis. You'd said you would still be in Lisbon when I returned—I could not believe you'd have left with no more than those few words. The clothing was there, but not Teresa, no sign of Shadrach. I thought perhaps you had gone to a party, but evening clothes were there and no invitation on Dalmonte's list . . ."

I shivered, imagining him striding from one empty room to another, anguished by uncertainty. His hand gripped mine tightly. "I called Figaro and Pernota, Navigaciones, Tavares . . . but my pride would not let me call any personal friends. At last I thought you might be at the house, so I went there. Joao said he'd seen you two days ago, and Teresa was on holiday with Shadrach at Santarém. Then I thought: she has gone to see Dorica or Juana Valdes. It was only ten o'clock.

"Shall I confess? I was quite calmed, reassured to the point that I inspected the house at leisure. I had no doubt that when, finally, I should return to the apartment, I should find you at home, where I would quickly convince you to remain. I was so sure of myself, *querida*," he said, sadly. "I was even impatient with you for being absent at the precise moment I wished to see you!

"So I seated myself at the new desk, I made various telephone calls, until I reached da Velma and learned you were here." He groaned, laying his forehead against my hand. "After what I'd learned from Rouland, I was terrified for you, Persis! I came as quickly as possible, but every mile was a nightmare, particularly when Rouland said Lariscos and Miguel had left in the helicopter."

"Please, couldn't we talk about something else?" I

murmured, wistfully. "Did you approve the house?"

"It is perfect," Seb made an effort. "It even feels different."

"It didn't cost a hundred thousand—and there aren't any doors between our dressing rooms," I said, experimentally.

"The better to fill those nurseries . . ."

"Dona Benedecta?"

Seb's jaw tightened. "She has retired to Agueda Verde," he said, evenly. "Legal action might be difficult, but as Rouland told her, a court action would be a *cause célèbre,* even if nothing were proved. Branca has gone to see her comfortably settled."

"Will Branca come to Lisbon, later?" I whispered.

"When I told her of the rooms you had prepared for her, she wept." He smiled at me tenderly. "Oh, the house is as transparent as your affections, dearest! One has only to walk through it to know who will inhabit each room. Branca asked me to give you her love, and to say there will be time enough for everything.

"She's known, suspected, for years; she dared do nothing. The least violence—no more than a slap— might have detached the retina again, left her blind forever. If only she'd confided in me, but she 'feared to intrude her personal problems when I was always so occupied with business.' " Seb's voice trembled, then steadied with effort. "I have been a poor brother, too, you see, but you will help me to make amends. She has nothing, not even legal status. The contents of the storeroom technically belong to Dorica, since her mother and grandmother placed them there; Miguel's real wife will be legally advised to make no claim.

"There is also the matter of Branca's dowry, and

the property at Agueda Grande," he finished. "We must see how Dorica views the affair. She is under no obligation to restore Miguel's share."

I thought about it. "She will," I decided, "and Branca will adopt her emotionally. I must transfer my inheritance from Uncle Ted, too. It isn't a great deal, but at least she and Pedro can be married at once."

Seb laughed helplessly. "There'll be a minor sensation when Dorica's proved legitimate, but I put nothing past you, *minha mulher*. You revolutionized my office, my business, my whole life, inside of twenty-four hours. Introducing the Revascues bastard to Lisbon society will be whipped cream in your hands." He stood up, stretching wearily. "Shall we return to Lisbon, or would you like to rest until tomorrow?"

I thought about that. I was suddenly wild to be in our own home, but Seb had driven half the night, been plunged into tragedy and violent nerve strain. "Isn't it too tiresome for you, dearest?"

"Nothing will ever be too tiresome again, *queridinho*, so long as I have you. You would prefer Lisbon?"

"Yes, please—but I haven't any clothes," I gulped, remembering that everything I'd brought with me had been in the Porsche, had been burned . . .

"If we find a coat, do you object to drive in the bathrobe?"

"You can wrap me in a blanket, like an Indian squaw."

"Ah? Come, there is not a moment to lose!" He was striding to the bell pull, flinging open doors, issuing orders, bellowing decrees. "Prepare the car, pack clothing for Dom Duarte, place a call to my office in Lisbon, find a coat for Dona Persis—we leave at once."

I lay still, watching him create an organized bustle. When he came back, "I'm admiring you, *meu coraçao.* You're so towering tall."

"All the Plantagenets were tall," he said, surprised. "Roberto, give us a thermos of milk, a bottle of claret, sandwiches, fruit . . ."

Well, I'm not the daughter of a history professor for nothing. "You mean, you're one of John o'Gaunt's calling cards?" I demanded, sliding out of bed and staring at him indignantly. "Dammit, what a sell! All I have is a Salem witch, and now you turn up a Plantagenet bastard."

Seb put hands on hips, standing in the doorway, and threw back his head in a shout of laughter. Behind him there was a gentle chuckle. "Do not lose your perspective, Dona Persis," Father Paul advised, placidly stroking Shadrach who was purring an oratorio. "The Plantagenets are dead, after all—but it appears an impossibility to kill a Salem witch."

Duarte sat next to me, holding Shadrach and buckled into my seat belt. Seb drove like the wind, as usual; I described New England, Andover, and my family to Duarte, in glowing terms and using English. Occasionally I corrected pronunciation, but the boy's command was good. "Explain this Appomattox, if you please," Seb suggested, poker-faced.

"Appomattox?" Duarte frowned, digging around in his mind. "It is a courthouse, *pia,* where the American Civil War ended." There was a minute pause, while Seb hurled us around a curve, but I beat him to the punch.

"Aha, you are intelligent, Duarte," I praised him blandly. "Do you know that your father thought it was 'an Appomattox,' and probably an American version of a machete?" Duarte's childish giggle rang out joyously, but Seb was equally bland.

"But a man always hopes his son will be smarter than he was . . ."

We stopped once for the requirements of nature; we stopped at sunset among trees with a view of the Tagus and demolished the rations in the wicker picnic basket provided by Roberto: cold chicken, thin meat sandwiches, tomatoes, hard boiled eggs, with tidbits for Shadrach, milk for Duarte, wine for adults. Then we were off again, sucking fresh oranges and peaches. The hell with how much juice dribbled over our chins. Above us, night conquered day in a brilliance of stars. Seb turned on the headlights and the car radio. We sang: Volare, The Girl from Ipanema, assorted flamenco and yeah-yeah-yeahs, very boisterous, highly inaccurate, but to our entire satisfaction. Duarte, Shadrach and I snoozed briefly—and suddenly the car was stationary.

Drowsily, I opened my eyes, aware of fingers loosening the seat belt. "Duarte, take Shadrach and slide out this side." Above were lights, an open door, Teresa and Joao smiling broadly, while Seb gently picked me up, still in my bathrobe, and carried me up the steps to the entrance hall. A youngster (who was Joao in essence, unquestionably a grandson) was scurrying up with Duarte's bags, rushing away to transfer the Ghia to its quarters. Duarte was starry-eyed with excitement, Shadrach was greeting Teresa with enthusiasm, and the chandelier still had to be raised, but Seb merely stood to one side while Joao quietly shut the front door.

"We are home, beloved?" he asked, hopefully.

"Now and forever, *meu marido* . . ."

GOTHIC MYSTERIES
of Romance and Suspense ...

by Rae Foley

A CALCULATED RISK
DARK INTENT
FATAL LADY
GIRL ON A HIGH WIRE
THE HUNDREDTH DOOR
MALICE DOMESTIC
THE MAN IN THE SHADOW
OMINOUS STAR
SCARED TO DEATH
THIS WOMAN WANTED
WILD NIGHT

and Velda Johnston

ALONG A DARK PATH
THE FACE IN THE SHADOWS
THE HOUSE ABOVE HOLLYWOOD
I CAME TO A CASTLE
THE LIGHT IN THE SWAMP
THE PEOPLE ON THE HILL
THE PHANTOM COTTAGE

Dell Books 75¢

If you cannot obtain copies of these titles from your local bookseller, just send the price (plus 15c per copy for handling and postage) to Dell Books, Post Office Box 1000, Pinebrook, N. J. 07058.

How many of these Dell Bestsellers have you read?